LOVE [illegible] THINGS

A CRYSTAL LAKE NOVEL

JULIANA STONE

Cover design by J.A. Stone

CHAPTER ONE

Beck Jacobs was not a cat guy.

In thirty-four years of living, he couldn't recall ever having any kind of moment with a cat. He'd always been team canine, and if life wasn't so busy, he'd have one of his own. And not one of those small yappy things either. He'd take a shepherd like the one his pal Jack owned, or a golden retriever like Taser from next door. That animal knew when his owner needed a beer and could open the fridge and get one on his own. As far as Beck was concerned, dogs were smarter than most humans he knew.

He thought about that as he got down on his back and worked his way underneath his truck, because dogs didn't do stupid things like hide inside the mechanics of an F-150.

The ground beneath him was snow covered, and it only took a few moments for the cold to seep through the red-and-black flannel shirt he'd pulled on over his jeans. His hair was still damp from the shower and icing up, and he'd run out so fast, he'd not bothered to button his shirt or grab a coat. With no socks in his hastily pulled on boots, it wouldn't take long before his toes were stubs of ice.

Five minutes ago, his morning had been stellar. He'd been up early for a Sunday because he had plans to finish the trim work in the kitchen on his current remodel, a small bungalow on a ravine lot in town, and was expected at his brother's place for dinner after a game of shinny with the guys. He downed two coffees and read the weekend paper (no online news for him) before the sun came up, and then he'd gone for a run. After a quick shower, he'd pressed the remote start on his key fob to warm up the truck while he got dressed, because damn, it was cold outside. Weather in Crystal Lake in March was iffy, and the last few days, it was a balmy thirty degrees.

He'd taken exactly two steps away from the front door when he spied a small, fluffy orange tail dangling from under the front of his truck. And now here he was, staring up at engine parts and wheel wells, looking for the little bastard.

"Where are you?" he muttered, squinting upward in the direction of a faint meow. He couldn't see shit and should have grabbed a flashlight, which was a good idea, and he rolled back out from underneath the truck and rummaged through the toolbox in the back of it. When he had the flashlight in hand, he got into position again, and, after a few moments, spotted two small green eyes staring down at him.

Beck spent the next five minutes trying to cajole the little guy from his perch, but it was a no-go. He angled his head for a look at his watch and swore. He was late.

"Come on, you little shit," he said under his breath as he reached his hand up, only to be rewarded by a sharp claw and a hiss.

"Excuse me. Is this a bad time?"

The voice came from nowhere and startled Beck. His body jerked, he slammed his head against metal and swore a blue streak, though he didn't take his eyes off the kitten. He'd been so damn close.

"Are you Beck?"

He swore.

"Hello?"

"Hold on," he all but growled, wincing as pain flared along his forehead.

"I don't mean to bother you. I'm just—"

"Dammit, give me a minute. Does it look like I'm in the position to have a conversation?" Something dripped into his eye, most likely blood, and if looks could kill, the woman, whoever the heck she was, would be a puddle of goop in the middle of his driveway.

"You don't need to be rude."

"Lady, I don't know who you are, and I sure as hell can't see you, but I'm going to assume you have two eyes in your head. I've got a bit of a situation here."

This damn cat would be the end of him.

"By all means, take care of your situation first," the voice replied, heavy with sarcasm. Beck scowled. He was cold, pissed off, still wet from the shower, and the damn cat was playing games.

Beck glared up at the puffball, which had crawled farther up between the wheel well and the engine block. "Come on, you little bastard," he muttered, reaching up as far as he could, shaking his head when he was rewarded with a hiss and another swipe of a tiny paw.

"Do you need help?" There was that damn voice again.

"Not from you." he barked. Who the hell was this woman?

He mentally willed the kitten to drop into his outstretched palm and, when that didn't happen, tried talking to it the way Jack talked to his kid, which basically sounded like gibberish. It didn't work, and those green eyes did nothing but stare down at him, the kitten taunting him with the odd soft meow. And now his day, which had started out so promising, was shot to hell and he'd be lucky to get to any of the trim done at the remodel.

He thought of calling his brother Nate and asking to borrow his truck, since he couldn't drive off with the kitten stuck inside of his. But then he thought of the cold and how small the little guy looked, and he didn't want it to freeze to death. Lord knows Nate's lady, Molly, the local vet, would hand him his ass if anything happened to the kitten.

"*Come on*," he said softly, wiggling his fingers a bit. The kitten leaned forward and sniffed around the edges of his fingernails, but when Beck leaned closer, it retreated. "You're going to freeze to death, buddy."

"What's up in there?"

This woman wasn't leaving anytime soon. Beck grimaced and pushed his way out from underneath the truck. He didn't bother to hide his scowl. "A kitten." He glanced up, but the sun was behind whoever stood a few inches from him, and he got to his feet. Her features came into focus as he moved a bit and his eyes got used to the brightness.

Creamy skin, high cheekbones, and a full mouth. Long dark hair and darker eyes that looked him up and down without giving anything away. Beck had no idea who she was, but the woman was treading on thin ice. He didn't have time for her bullshit.

"Are you all right?" She pointed to his head, which throbbed.

"I'll be fine once I know who you are and why you're here." He rubbed his hands together to keep them warm, then took the edge of his shirt and swiped at the blood that dripped from the gash on his forehead. What the actual fu—

"I'm Sid Bennett. I'm renting a place on the lake and was told to pick up the key from someone named Beck at this address." Her chin jutted out defiantly. "Are you Beck?"

Shit. That was today? Beck bought the stone cottage last year with the notion of flipping it, but once the project was done, he'd decided to keep the place and use it as a rental property. It was his greatest flaw, his inability to get rid of things. In the last five years, he'd flipped six or seven homes and managed to make a very good living doing it. But when a man puts his heart and soul and sweat into a project, he leaves a piece of himself behind when he walks away from it.

Beck had a hard time walking away.

He focused on the woman, Sid, and his eyebrows shot up. "I wasn't expecting you until tomorrow." That last conversation with Nate was coming back to him.

"I was able to get away earlier than I expected to, and Nate said it wouldn't be a problem."

"Did he now." A heads-up would have been nice.

"Is it a problem?"

"No," he replied sharply, more irritated than he should be. A sharp wail, like the little kitten's lungs were being squeezed out of him, ripped through the quiet. It damn near made the hair on the back of Beck's neck stand on end. Dammit to hell, but he didn't have time for this. He swore under his breath.

"Do you want me to try?"

He looked her over real good. The woman was dressed in a white wool coat that fell to just above the knee. Her leather boots were a pale tan color, and the emerald scarf around her neck was silk. Beck might not know much, but it didn't take a rocket scientist to know the coat alone cost more than all the clothes hanging in his closet. She looked like a city girl and sounded like the West Coast, and he searched his mind for more information. But either Nate hadn't elaborated when he first approached Beck about the rental, or, more likely, Beck hadn't paid attention.

There wasn't much that interested him lately, aside from work.

"Knock yourself out." He stepped aside and gave her some room.

She walked back to the expensive SUV parked a few feet away from his truck and rummaged around a bit, then returned clutching a pink-and-black bag. She opened it and popped a candy in her mouth and smiled at him. The smile wasn't the kind that invited one in return, so he didn't bother. It was made of ice and about as frosty as the look in her eyes.

"I know what you're thinking," she said.

He was thinking that she looked good bent over the front seat of her vehicle, which should have surprised him considering she wasn't his type. But then, since Cate, he hadn't looked at anyone in a way that mattered.

"I doubt that."

"You're thinking, no way can I get that little kitten to come to me when you've been trying for the last hour."

"Fifteen minutes."

"What?"

"I'd be a popsicle if I'd been out here for an hour."

Her eyes dropped to his bare chest, and for a ghost of a moment, he noticed the pink in her cheeks deepened.

"You're a little underdressed for the weather."

"I'm just out of the shower. Damn cat is lucky I noticed it when I started the truck."

"May I?" She moved past him and leaned toward the truck and shook the bag, all the while speaking softly to the kitten. Within seconds, *literal seconds,* the small fur ball appeared, meowing loudly, as it jumped up toward the bag, those sharp little claws extended like daggers. She scooped up the kitten and turned to Beck, her hands outstretched. The fur ball looked smaller than any kitten Beck had ever seen before. When he didn't immediately take the little guy from her, she frowned.

"This belongs to you."

"I don't like cats."

"Well, it was in your truck."

"I don't like cats," he repeated.

Her eyes narrowed. "You don't have a choice."

She moved closer and held up the kitten, and Beck gave her the stink eye before he grabbed hold of it. Oil and dirt left marks on its orange face and back, but other than that, the animal seemed okay, though it was shivering something fierce. Beck held the kitten against his chest and pulled one half of his flannel shirt over it for warmth. It immediately began to purr, an odd sensation, but not exactly unpleasant.

"Can I have the key now?"

He looked at the woman and nodded toward his house. The sooner she got the key, the sooner she'd be out of his hair and he could deal with the cat. "I'll grab it for you." She followed him inside, and he held the kitten gingerly while rooting through the pile of paperwork on the kitchen table that, at the moment, doubled as his workstation. He found the envelope marked *stone cottage* and handed it over.

"You out here on your own?" he asked.

"How is that any of your business? A woman can't rent a home on her own?" Her sharp tone got his attention. Another time and place, he might have wondered about it, but as it was, he had his own personal shit to deal with and had no desire to get involved with anyone else's. Especially some prickly woman from the West Coast with a chip on her shoulder.

"I don't give a rat's ass about your situation," he replied. "I just wondered if you needed an extra key. I only have the one, but can get a spare made up for you."

Her eyes slid from his. "I'm fine with the one."

"Good. The cottage is just up the road," he said as she took the key. "Technically, the next property over, but my place here is about ten acres, so it's a bit of a hike."

"Thanks." She backed away.

"The heat and hot water aren't on. I didn't get a chance to get up there because—"

"I'm early. Trust me, I got that."

"There's a file on the kitchen island with all the instructions you need."

She pointed to his chest. "I'm not sure who to feel sorry for." She paused. "You or the cat."

She closed the door, and Beck watched through the window as she slid into her shiny SUV and, moments later, drove away. He'd been a dick, no doubt about that, but then he'd probably never see her again, so what did it matter?

He groped for his cell phone, and Nate picked up on the first ring. "Two things," he said before his brother could say hello.

"What's that?"

"Your friend is early."

"Sid?"

"That's the one."

"Good to know. What's the other one?"

Beck looked down at the kitten tucked into his flannel, now fast asleep and purring like a machine. He should drop it at Molly's animal shelter and let them deal with it, because he didn't have time for a cat. Hell, he didn't even like them.

Not really.

Just then, the kitten stretched and slowly opened its green eyes. For a moment, it felt like the little fur ball could see right into his soul. The kitten angled its head and snuggled closer before resuming purring and kneaded the edge of his shirt with its paws.

"Beck?"

Don't do it.

Beck leaned against the counter in his kitchen and sighed. "What do you feed a kitten?"

CHAPTER TWO

The stone cottage was perfect.

Sid fingered the file folder on the dove-gray island and was about to take a tour of the place when her cell phone shrilled, breaking the silence with all the subtlety of a rock through glass. Sid knew who it was on account of the ring-tone—Garth Brooks and *Friends in Low Places* was her sister's anthem. It was barely eight a.m. in San Diego, but the fact her sister was up shouldn't surprise Sid. With a sigh, she pulled out her phone, because if she didn't answer, Kylie would call back again and *again* until she did.

"Hey," Sid said, walking over to the large double windows that overlooked the backyard, beyond which was Crystal Lake. It was still snow-covered as far as she could see. She blinked at the brilliance of it all as the sun reflected back at her.

"When were you going to tell me you skipped town?" Kylie's husky voice was sharp in her ear, but Sid didn't get a chance to respond. "Your phone was turned off, so I had to call your assistant, and she told me you left town. I called to confirm lunch. Did you forget about that? Lunch on the pier with Jordan and the girls? Where the hell are you?"

Damn. She'd totally spaced on lunch. Sid rubbed the bridge of her nose as fingers of pain sliced through her skull. The headache would be epic unless she dealt with it. She headed back to the kitchen.

"I'm in Crystal Lake." She rummaged through her bag and found some pain meds, which she popped into her mouth and swallowed dry. "And I didn't skip town. That would imply I've done something wrong."

"Running away from your problems *is* wrong."

"Don't start," Sid replied, rolling her eyes at the ceiling.

"Where the hell is Crystal Lake anyway?"

"Kylie, do we really have to do this right now? I just got here, and have a million things to do." That was a lie. The only thing she had planned was to relax and then head to Nate's for dinner.

"Yes, we have to do this right now. My lunch plans are canceled, remember? So I have all the time in the world to get into it with you. Someone sure as hell needs to."

"Kylie."

"Where is Crystal Lake?"

Sid stared out the windows at the perfect scene before her. It was March, but there was still so much of winter left here.

"Michigan."

"You're in Michigan? Why?"

"Because I needed to get away, and I needed to be on my own." She closed her eyes. "It's been too much. This past year and everything that happened. I'm trying to get through it, but sometimes it feels like I'm slogging my way through quicksand and barely able to keep my head above it. I just..." She slumped against a cream sofa and shrugged, staring at her reflection in the window. "I need to not remember, and it's hard to not remember when I'm home," she whispered.

"But, Sid—"

"No, Kylie. Just...no. You mean well, I know that, but you're suffocating me. I feel like I can't breathe. Like all of you are watching and waiting for me to fall apart. It's exhausting."

Silence greeted her confession.

"Kylie?"

"I'm sorry. I didn't know I made you feel that way." Her sister's voice was small, and Sid heard the hurt there. It made Sidney feel like crap. She stared out at the brilliant sun on the diamond-encrusted snow until it blurred. Would her life ever be normal again? Would she be able to look through the shadows that clung to the corners of her mind? Would she be able to forget?

"I appreciate you wanting to be there for me. I really do. But I need to face some things on my own. I had to get away, Ky, and no one knows me here. I can breathe without anyone watching. I know you mean the best and that you care about me, but I need to be away from everyone right now. I can't explain it any other way."

"Promise me something?" Kylie asked softly.

"Anything."

"When you're done facing all those ghosts alone, will you call me?"

"I will."

"I mean it, Sidney. You might think you need to be alone, but until you're deep in it, you won't know."

"Won't know what?"

"That you're wrong. Call me, and I'll be on the first plane out. I love you."

Sid said her goodbye and tossed her cell back onto the counter. She shrugged out of her wool coat and then stepped out of her boots. She'd brought a weekender bag, which sat by the front door, and scooped it up, glancing between the hall just off the kitchen and the stairs by the entrance. She quickly made her way down the hall and peeked in at a farmhouse-style bathroom, including a shower, and two smaller rooms, one a bedroom done up in cream and navy blue, the other an office or library-type space with a pullout sofa.

The main area of the cottage, which included the kitchen, dining area, and family room, was open and airy—there weren't any more rooms hiding in there, so she headed to the stairs, figuring the master bedroom was up there. They brought her to a beautiful loft dominated by a king-size bed along a wall of exposed bleached gray stone. The ceiling was crisscrossed with huge dark wood beams, the wood flooring restored to warm perfection, the whitewashed walls a perfect accent. Two skylights let in a ton of natural light, and there was a seating area across from the bed in front of a fireplace with an overstuffed cream chair, a steel-blue throw across one arm, and comfy white accent pillows. A walk-in closet big enough for two and a large bathroom complete with a luxurious tub in front of a window that overlooked the lake took up the rest of the space. The bathtub was copper, an antique, with claw legs, and deeper than any she'd ever seen.

If it wasn't for the fact the hot water wasn't on yet, she'd have filled the sucker immediately and soaked away her worries. But she needed to take care of a few things first. Sid headed back downstairs and grabbed the file folder from the kitchen. It didn't take long to find the furnace and hot water tank, both located in the basement, and an hour later, she'd unpacked and was soaking in a tub full of steaming-hot water. She leaned back, closed her eyes, and eventually drifted off. If any of the ghosts from her past came calling, she didn't hear them knock, because when she finally woke up, it was hours later, the water was cold, and, for the first time in a long time, she felt rested.

Because she was a day early, Nate hadn't been able to fill the fridge or the pantry, which he'd planned on doing. Instead, she was invited to dinner, and if she didn't get her butt in gear, she'd be late.

With her stomach rumbling, 'cause Lord knows she couldn't remember the last time she ate, Sid pulled on a pair of deep-blue tights and an oversized Giants hoodie and slipped into a pair of boots. She pulled her hair into a loose topknot, grabbed her keys and phone, and headed outside.

The sun was still in the sky, though it hung low, and the air was crisp. Underneath her feet, snow crunched, and it took a bit for her SUV to heat up. Next time, she'd be smart and start it from inside the cottage. As she shivered in the driver's seat waiting for the defrost to work its magic, she thought of Beck and the kitten and wondered how he'd made out.

Then she felt silly wondering about a guy who was rude as hell and headed onto River Road in the opposite direction from his place. Nathan's home was about ten minutes away according to her GPS, and when she pulled into the driveway marked Manchester House, it took a bit for Sid to let the beauty sink in. This wasn't just a house, it was an estate, probably built by wealthy landowners long ago.

The home was old—from the design and materials, she'd say mid-1800s—and set on a clearing that overlooked the lake and was surrounded by trees, evergreens, and oak, to name a few. To her right was an outbuilding that looked as if it could have been a stable at one time, and there was another smaller building up the hill beyond it.

She was about to step out of the SUV when the front door flew open and Nate appeared, a big smile on his face, his arm around his wife, Molly, who was pregnant with twins. For a moment, Sid's eyes settled on the woman, and such a feeling of longing washed over her that she had to take a few more seconds before she exited the vehicle.

"Molly, you look beautiful," she said, giving the woman a

hug before doing the same to the man at her side. She'd only met Molly once, in New York just after Christmas, but they'd instantly bonded and had kept up a friendship via text message and FaceTime.

Molly stepped back and rubbed her belly. "Well, thanks for that. Growing twins is exhausting." She smiled. "I'm so glad you decided to come and spend some time here." Molly's eyes softened. "It's God's country, and nothing is better for the soul than Crystal Lake."

"How's the cottage?" Nate asked, ushering her inside.

"Oh my God, Nathan, it's...I don't have words. Honestly, I couldn't have asked for a more gorgeous place to stay, and this..." Sidney turned in a full circle, and sighed in pleasure. "It's been a long time since I've walked into a home that blends the old and new so well." The woodwork was incredible, the original floors gleamed, and even the light fixtures were an ode to the past. "You have a beautiful home."

They headed to the back of the large house, where the kitchen was a dream of white and green and light, with dark stainless-steel appliances that were obviously new, but retro in style. The focal point, a large granite island with generous seating, opened up to a family room.

"Something smells good," Sid said as she took a seat at the island.

Molly poured her a glass of red wine at about the same time a gangly golden dog with white spots and long legs it hadn't grown into came from nowhere and nearly upended Nathan.

"This must be Petal," Sid said, eyeing up the dog. "She's going to be huge. You know that, right?"

"Yeah." Nate grinned and kissed the dog on the nose. "But she'll always be my baby."

Molly rolled her eyes and laughed, ambling over to her husband in that way that pregnant women do. She snuggled into his arms, raised her face for a kiss, and Sidney couldn't help but see the love these two had for each other.

Why do some people find this and others don't?

The question burned in her mind, and she looked away, ashamed at her thoughts. She was happy for Nate and Molly, of course she was, but she was also jealous and angry and so very sad at the thought she would never have what they did.

She pasted a smile to her face when Petal bounded around the corner of the island and sniffed around her feet, which lasted only a few seconds before something else caught her attention and the dog disappeared as quick as she'd come.

The three of them munched on veggies and hummus, Sid and Nate got started in on the wine, while Molly had sparkling water. They didn't talk about anything too deep, and thankfully, neither Molly nor Nate delved into her reason for coming to Crystal Lake. Nate had been a good friend, and he knew things she'd asked him not to share. From what she could tell, he'd honored his promise.

"You got into the cottage with no issues?" Molly asked.

Sid nodded. "The hot water and heat weren't on, but that was my fault being a day early and all." She made a face. "Something your pal Beck didn't seem to like."

Molly's eyes widened. "Really?"

"Oh yeah." Sidney drained her wineglass, liking the slow buzz it brought, and held it up for another. "He might look good half-dressed holding on to a kitten, but he sure as hell isn't someone I'd choose to spend time with. I know his type. He's too good-looking for his own good, with an inflated sense of self, and his manners are crap."

"That doesn't sound like Beck," Molly replied, sounding a tad strained. Which Sidney would have caught if she hadn't downed two large glasses of wine on an empty stomach. As it was, she was distracted, though she caught a strange look pass between Nate and Molly. She was just about to comment on it when Petal began to bark and whine, followed by the sound of the front door closing and the stomping of heavy boots.

Sid swung around on her stool and looked at the doorway. "You expecting company?" she asked, looking over her shoulder at Nate.

"My brother."

Sid frowned. Okay. She knew there was a story here, but for the life of her, she couldn't nail it down.

"I hope you don't mind," Molly said, a panicked look on her face as she slowly made her way around the island to stand beside Sid.

"No. Why would I?" Sidney's puzzled frown deepened. She opened her mouth to ask about their guest when a familiar voice drew her attention back to the kitchen doorway.

The guy who'd given her the key to the cottage, the guy she knew as Beck, stood with Nate and gave him a hug, his smile wide and open and pretty damn devastating if a girl was interested. No scowling there. Nope. He saved that for Sid, apparently.

He looked up suddenly and caught her eye, and his smile disappeared like ghosts melting into the shadows.

"What's she doing here?"

He glanced from Nathan to her, and then back to Nate again, his features hard, his eyes glittering and dark.

"I thought this was a family dinner." His voice was biting.

Seriously? The man with the key was Nate's brother?

Sidney set down her wineglass and glanced at Nate. She didn't know how to act because the words that sat on the tip of her tongue were not nice. Not only did his manners leave a lot to be desired, but the guy was an arrogant piece of work.

"Normally when you walk into a house, you start off with a greeting." Nathan glared at his brother. "Like, 'hello' or 'nice to meet you.' You're lucky Mom isn't here, because she sure as hell would set you straight." Nate glanced her way. "You've already met Sidney, someone I've known for a long time, and I invited her for dinner. There is no agenda, so wipe that look off your face, apologize to Sid for being a prick, and grab a beer."

Sid snuck a look at Molly for help. Agenda? What did Nate mean by that?

Beck muttered something under his breath, and Sid was pretty sure it was aimed at her. "The last time I showed up for dinner, one of your *friends* was sitting right where she is. She had more arms than a damn octopus and showed up at my house the next day with a dozen muffins." He sounded disgusted. "I don't like muffins, and I sure as hell didn't like her."

"Oh, you don't have to worry about that," Sid piped up, more than a little insulted. "I don't like to bake." She swirled the wine in her glass. "And I've only got two arms, I promise."

His gaze swung her way, and for a moment, it felt as if they were the only two people in the room. Her heartbeat filled her ears, and she wasn't aware she'd held her breath until it fell out of her in a long sigh.

"Okay, then." Nathan shook his head, clearly exasperated. "Now that we know Beck's not in danger of waking up to fresh-baked muffins tomorrow morning, can we start over?"

CHAPTER THREE

Dinner was a disaster, and Beck was more than willing to take responsibility for it because he'd set the tone. The entire evening had been a subdued affair, definitely not the norm for Nate and Molly's place.

He sure as hell didn't blame Sidney Barrett for bailing five minutes after the plates were cleared. She'd claimed fatigue and a long travel day and, after hugging Nathan and Molly, nodded his way, a quick, polite sort of thing before she disappeared into darkness.

It was more than Beck deserved.

"You got anything you need to talk about?" Nathan asked from across the kitchen where he was loading up the dishwasher. "Some *thing* that's got you acting like a complete asshole?"

Molly, working overtime growing two babies in her belly, plunked her butt onto the sofa a few feet away and looked at him, a thoughtful expression on her face.

"Beck thinks we're trying to set him up with Sid," Molly said. "And your brother doesn't like being set up."

"Not this again." Nathan tossed a tea towel over his shoulder and shook his head.

"You guys have a track record for putting me on the spot. No way you can deny it." Beck shoved his hands into the front pockets of his jeans. "Two days after Christmas it was Angela Smith."

"Hey, in my defense I thought you liked her." Nate shrugged and leaned against the island.

"Just because I cleared the snow from her driveway doesn't mean I want to date the woman."

"You cleared her driveway every day for two weeks." Nate wasn't giving in.

"Because Gus Aldridge, the guy who normally does it, was in Florida with his family and asked me to."

"Oh." Nate had nothing for that.

"And then there was Danielle Evans on New Year's Eve. She came at me like a barracuda. By the end of the evening, she was planning a vacation together. Seriously. That woman has more baggage than anyone I know, and she wants to go to Cabo with me? What's your excuse there?" Beck looked his brother straight in the eye.

"I don't have one other than the fact you've been such a grouchy bastard lately, I figured you needed to get laid."

"*Nathan.*" Molly struggled to turn around and glare at his brother.

"What?" Nate shrugged. "It's true. You said so yourself."

Molly sank back onto the sofa, those all-seeing eyes of hers back on Beck. She had the humility to look at least a little embarrassed. "You have seemed a little on edge." She sighed. "Look, we love you, and we're worried about you. That's all." Her eyes shifted to Nate and then back to him. "You don't seem happy."

"I'm fine," he replied darkly. "Not everybody needs to live a world overflowing with goddamn unicorns."

"What's wrong with unicorns?" Nathan's attempt to lighten things went unnoticed because Molly wasn't giving up.

"You work most every day, sometimes until midnight. You play hockey with the boys one night a week in the winter or baseball in the summer and come here for dinner every other Sunday. But that's it. You have no life outside of whatever house it is you're working on, or a couple of social beers at the Coach House. It's not healthy to be that closed off from the rest of the world." Molly said the words in a rush.

Beck took a step back because he knew where they were headed, and the last thing he wanted to do was discuss his personal situation with anyone, let alone his brother Nate, a guy who currently had the world by the balls.

Nathan perched on the edge of the sofa and looked up at Beck. The look in his brother's eyes made Beck uncomfortable. "I know you don't like talking about Cate, but—"

"Don't," he all but growled.

"It's been over ten years. We all know how much you loved her. We all did too. I mean, that girl was part of our family. But Beck, she'd want you to be happy. Don't you think it's time to move on?"

Beck clamped his jaw tight, and it took a bit for him to work his way up to saying a few words. He grabbed his jacket and shrugged into it, then took another few moments before he turned back to Molly and Nate.

He loved them; they were family. But they didn't get it. The day that son of a bitch drunk driver took her away from him was the day he knew his life would never be the same. Because what he and his fiancée had had was the kind of thing that only comes around once in a lifetime. He had zero interest in anything less than that.

"What I think is that I'd appreciate it if the two of you would stay the hell out of my personal life. I'm fine." He looked at both of them. "If the state of my being *fine* doesn't exactly measure up to what both of you think it should or fall in line with your version of it, well, I got nothing but it is what it is." He held up his hand when Molly opened her mouth. "No, Molls. I know you've got the best of intentions, but trust me when I say I don't need this, okay? I'm not an addict. I don't need an intervention. I just need to be left alone."

Beck scooped up his jacket and headed for the front door. "Thanks for dinner. I hope I didn't ruin it."

By the time he got back to his place, snow was starting to fall again. The flakes were light and powdery, the kind that didn't stick but would disappear on the next gust of wind. Winter hung on with tenacious fingers; in like a lion, out like a lamb, or so they said. His house was dark, and he sat for a moment staring at it, shoulders tight with tension, mind heavy with thoughts he'd rather forget.

It was an old cottage he'd winterized, and he'd bought out here for the property, not the home. Truthfully, he'd hardly spent any time fixing up the house because he didn't care all that much about it. It was his base of operations, so to speak. In fact, he spent more time in the large shop he'd built for his business than he did in the house. For a guy who spent his living breathing new life into old homes, he wasn't sure what that said about him.

Beck thought about that for a bit, and then he got mad that he was thinking about it and hopped out of his truck in a rush. He strode inside the house and was immediately hit by a small, vibrating ball of fur that purred so loudly, he was amazed at the sound such a small animal could produce.

It was unbelievable, but he'd forgotten about the kitten.

Earlier, he'd set up a litter box, food, and water in the

mudroom where he'd left the little guy, but he must not have latched it properly. Beck scooped him up, and once he made sure the water was topped up and there was kibble in the bowl (he was glad to see the kitten had eaten), he closed the door and headed to his bedroom.

He tossed his clothes onto the chair in the corner of his room and, in his boxers, flopped onto the bed. He'd barely settled in when the kitten began to wail, its cries shrill in the dark and quiet. Beck gave it a couple of minutes, but if anything, the crying got louder.

"For fuck's sake," he muttered, rolling off the bed. When he opened the door to the mudroom, the kitten was on him like bees on honey, rubbing against his leg and purring and meowing up a storm. Those big green eyes stared up at him, and for the longest time, he did nothing but stare back. But then something shifted inside him, some little piece of his heart that gave in, and, knowing he'd probably regret his next action, Beck grabbed him up and headed back to his room.

He settled back against the pillows, and damned if the kitten didn't snuggle up under his chin and begin to purr loudly. The animal meowed occasionally, seemingly happy to feel safe and secure and warm, and somewhere in the night, the darn thing claimed a piece of Beck that he thought was dead. He didn't know it, of course, but he would. Eventually.

When he woke up, the kitten was still asleep, curled in the same position. Gingerly, Beck got to his feet, not wanting to disturb it. He tucked some blankets around him and had a quick shower, then dressed quickly in a pair of old jeans, work boots, and a faded black T-shirt. He didn't want to leave the kitten on the bed because it was a long way down for such a small thing, so he brought him into the kitchen and made a bed for him on one of the chairs while he brewed his coffee.

Outside, the sun was poking through the night sky while the

snow still fell and glistened. It was that perfect time of morning, that hour when most folks were asleep and the world was silent. Which was why he nearly jumped out of his skin when there was a knock at his door, followed by someone jangling the doorknob.

What the hell?

The kitten raised his head and looked over as Beck strode toward the door. He took a moment and peeked out the small window there, then opened the door to find his mother shivering in the early morning cold.

"Mom? What are you doing here? Is everything okay?" Instantly concerned, he stepped aside and hurried her in.

"I'm fine, Beckworth."

He winced at his Christian name, suddenly on alert. His mom only used it when she was either up to something or upset with him.

"Is that coffee I smell?" Her voice was light, seemingly unconcerned, so he was going to assume she was up to something.

She stepped out of her boots and shrugged off her bright red puffy jacket, mittens, and hat. He followed her over to the kitchen, where she came to a stop when she spied the kitten, now standing on the chair and giving them both a long stretch and leisurely twitch of its tail.

"Well, aren't you the cutest little thing. When did you get a kitten?" Elise Jacobs didn't bother to hide her surprise, or pleasure, for that matter, as she walked over to the chair and gently picked up the little orange fur ball. "Beck, she's adorable."

He wasn't going to debate the level of cuteness the kitten possessed with his mother. "I've been calling it a he, and don't get too attached because I doubt he'll be here the next time you show up at six in the morning."

Elise held it up, had a look, and shrugged. "It's hard to tell at this age. You'll have to get Molly to examine it and tell you the sex." She looked at Beck. "I think it's a girl." She cradled the kitten against her chest and waited for Beck to pour her coffee before following him to the sad red-and-black-plaid sofa in the living room. The furniture in here, not that there was much, had been pilfered from a renovation he'd worked on a few years back. The stuff was old and worn, but Beck didn't care—it served a purpose.

There wasn't a table for his mother to set her coffee on, so she let the cat free, and the little guy immediately began to play with the tassels on some old pillow someone had given Beck when he'd first moved in.

"Where'd you find the cat?" Elise asked, watching him closely.

Beck knew she had an ulterior motive for coming to his place, but he was fine with playing this game—at least until he was done with his coffee.

"He was hiding up inside my truck yesterday. Probably crawled up in there to keep warm. He's damn lucky I saw his tail, because it could have been game over if I hadn't."

"You got a name?"

"Nah. Like I said, I'm not keeping him."

"You said you were doubtful." His mom flashed a smile. "You should name him."

"You're up early." He changed the subject, something he'd learned to do from the best—his mom.

She nodded. "I have a list of things to do a mile long, so I was up and at 'em at five." She cracked a smile. "I've already been to the gym."

For the first time, he noticed her clothing, black-and-pink tights with a matching long-sleeve top. His eyebrows shot up. "Gym? That's impressive." His mother had always been a small thing. He would bet she'd never been much more than a buck twenty in her life. She'd never been particularly active—golfing was about it for her, and maybe the occasional hike along the lake. She drank soda at least once a day—and not the diet kind—loved chocolate and chips and fried chicken, and made no apologies for it. He'd heard her say on more than one occasion that she had her father to thank for an undeniably high metabolism.

"Doctor Hanley said I needed to get more exercise."

Beck frowned. "Why? Is something wrong?"

"Nothing a little cardio can't fix."

"That's not being specific at all." His sarcasm was strong, and he didn't need the look in his mother's eye to tell him. "Care to elaborate?"

"My sugar is creeping up, and my cholesterol is a tad high. That's all."

"I'm going to guess no more soda or chips either."

She made a face and sighed. "What's the point in living if I can't at least enjoy all the things I love?" She ticked the kitten under the chin, smiling when it flopped onto its back and stared up at her. "I mean, God put sour-cream-and-onion chips on this planet for a reason." She sat back and fixed her eyes on him. "But that's not why I came by, Beck."

Here it comes, he thought.

"I didn't think it was."

"Your father is turning sixty next month, Easter weekend, to be exact, and we need to plan something. I just wanted to put the bug in your ear. I'd like input from both of you boys."

Relief, fast and hard, washed over him. Elise Jacobs was like a dog with a bone when she set her sights on something, and he'd been in her sights before, several times, in fact, and it wasn't pretty.

Beck relaxed, rolled his neck, and sipped from his coffee mug. This wasn't about him.

"I talked to Nathan last night."

Beck sat a little straighter and narrowed his eyes because the look in hers had changed. She was good. Reeled him in, got him comfortable, did a bait and switch, and now she had him where she wanted him. "Did you."

"Uh-huh." She nodded and took a moment, those all-seeing eyes of hers not wavering. "You know we loved Cate like she was one of our own." No beating around the bush for this woman.

"Mom," he interrupted. "I don't want to do this with you. I really don't." He got to his feet.

"You're going to listen to me, Beckworth, and when I'm done, you can have your say." There was no give in her voice or eyes, so Beck crossed his arms over his chest and waited. This was his mother, after all, and that gave her more leeway than anyone else on the planet.

"I won't pretend to understand your grief, because it would be insulting if I did. I know a part of you died when that car hit her, and that piece is gone forever because it belonged to her. And wherever she is right now, she's holding fast to it as she should be. But the thing about your heart is that it eventually heals. Of course, there will be scar tissue, and that's a good thing because it means you've loved." She angled her head to the side and shrugged. "Now, maybe you're not meant to fall in love again. Maybe Cate is the only woman you'll ever love. I don't know. None of us knows." She took a moment, and Beck's arms tightened. He saw the pain in her eyes and felt it reflected in his own.

"But honey, you can't stop living just because she's gone. At some point, you need to open yourself up to at least the possibility of feeling that kind of connection again. Hiding in your work, staying out here for days on end when no one sees you, living in this house, which is in a state of controlled chaos, from what I can see... That's not healthy. We just want you to be happy, Beck. All of us." She sighed softly and curled her hands around the kitten. "Don't you want to belong to someone again? Don't you want a family? Don't you think that maybe you're looking at this wrong? That maybe someone out there needs you to complete them?"

Anger flared inside him. Anger that was always there, simmering under the skin. He chose his words carefully. "I had all that, everything you're talking about, until I didn't. Until Dave Matthews drank a case of beer and got behind the wheel of his truck. Until she was gone, and I got left behind. The thing you guys don't get is that life isn't like the movies. The guy doesn't always get the girl and the house and the kids and the dog." He took a moment to get his thoughts straight. "Look. Even if I met a woman I thought I could build some kind of life with, I wouldn't do it. I'd walk away."

"My God, Beck, why?" He saw the anguish in his mother's eyes.

"Because it wouldn't be fair. She'd be living in the shadow of someone she could never touch, and eventually, it would implode anyway, so why put someone through that kind of pain? I can't do that. You need to understand that there will never be another Cate, not for me. She was my soulmate, Mom. As dumb and cliché as that sounds, I can't explain it any other way. I barely made it through those first few years after she died. I was a mess. You were there. You saw. It was like I was underwater. Drowning. But once I realized that from that day I first laid eyes on her in sixth grade, right up until that last kiss an hour before she died...when I knew that would be all I'd have, that there'd be no more... That was a lightbulb moment. I was able to breathe again. I'm a realist, and I'm good. It might not be the kind of good you wanted for me, and it sure as hell isn't the kind of good I did either. But I'm getting through it the only way

I know how, and you and Dad and Nate need to get onboard, because I'm not having this conversation again. I'm sick of being set up with women I have no interest in other than a quick lay. Trust me, when I need to scratch that itch, I get it done on my own. There's no problems there."

Elise Jacobs was quiet for a few more moments and then slowly got to her feet. She wrapped Beck up in a tight hug and didn't let go for the longest time. When she did, she cleared her throat and grabbed her jacket. Once she had her boots and hat on, she paused at the door.

Beck didn't realize he'd been holding his breath until he let it out. He was still tense. Still waiting for the other shoe to drop, because his mother was, if anything, the type not to let go easily.

"Okay," she said softly. "But two more things." She nodded toward the living room. "Promise me you'll at least keep that cat. She found you for a reason."

Wasn't happening. "I'll think about it."

"And please give her a name."

Beck cracked a smile and relaxed.

"And Beck?" She reached for the doorknob.

"Yes?"

"Apologize to that girl from yesterday." She gave him a look. "Properly."

"Who?" he shot back quickly.

"Nathan's friend. He said you weren't very nice to her. I raised you better than to be a rude asshat, Beckworth. Make sure you apologize, because that's not something I'll let go."

Son of a bitch.

She got him again.

CHAPTER FOUR

By ten a.m., Sid was crawling the walls.

The night before, she'd fallen into bed exhausted, and for the first time in a long time hadn't needed any kind of sleep aid to get the job done. No pills or tea or oil. It was lights out for this girl about ten minutes after she'd come back from Nate's.

She was awake before it was light outside and spent a few lazy hours sipping coffee by the fireplace with the book she'd brought along. She caught the sunrise over Crystal Lake and had breakfast while it happened, enjoying the silence and solitude. This was what she'd needed. This was what she wanted. To refresh her batteries, get away from the city, forget about the mess she'd left behind, and disappear in a place where no one knew her.

A mental and physical break. Her doctor had been after her about it for weeks.

So it was kind of funny that a few hours in, all she wanted was to do *something*. She poked her head outside, inhaled a shot of fresh, crisp air, and decided a trip to town was in order, especially considering she needed groceries. Molly had sent her home with a few things the night before, but she still had to stock up. Besides, a walk around town would be fun.

An hour later, she'd showered and dressed in faded jeans and a pale pink sweater. Her makeup was light, a bit of gloss on her lips, a touch of mascara, and she pulled her hair up into a ponytail. She was pretty sure that even if she ran into folks who knew who Sid Barrett was, they wouldn't recognize the Crystal Lake version. She grabbed her brown leather Vuitton and a beige sweater and headed outside. It was still chilly, but the sun felt nice on her face, and her steps were light.

Only when she drove past Beck Jacobs's place did she think of him. Well, she'd had a few evil thoughts the night before, but they didn't count. She snuck a look and saw his truck was gone, and then decided that Beck wasn't worth the stress he created. The man had issues, no way around that, and complicated seemed too light a word to use in conjunction with him.

Sid had left complicated behind her, along with a pile of pain and heartbreak. She needed to focus on herself and not think about a man who was rude and cold and had zero manners or social skills.

Even if he was dangerously handsome, in a rugged, wholly male kind of way.

For one second in her mind's eye, she saw Beck half-dressed with his shirt hanging open, cradling that kitten, and, in spite of herself, shook her head and exhaled. He was the kind of man to set most women's hearts fluttering a mile a minute, even someone like Sid, a woman whose heart was no longer whole. But in the end, it didn't matter. *He* didn't matter because Sid was a lost cause.

Only a fool would get involved with her. Or someone as screwed up as she was.

The drive to town took about fifteen minutes. She drove past a grocery store on the outskirts of town because she wanted to explore a bit before she ran her errand. A lovely park was central to the town center, there along a riverbank, and she parked in a municipal lot, eyes on a cute boardwalk that sported a host of shops and boutiques.

An old caboose had been converted into a food joint and was open, selling hot chocolate, among other things, out of a take-out window. Sid grabbed a large with extra marshmallows, sipping it lazily as she slowly made her way down the path that followed the river. It was warmer than the day before in spite of the snow on the ground, and with the sun on her face, she felt spring in the air.

Mothers and toddlers smiled as they went by, as did the odd jogger—she supposed most folks were at work on this fine Monday morning. A walking club consisting of elderly folks dressed in bright green matching track suits with neon-yellow hats came at her from the opposite direction, all in sync, but with generous smiles and waves as they passed by.

She spied a boutique called Bella & Hooch across the way, with lovely throws in the display window, and headed there. She could use one for mornings with her book. There were a few customers inside chatting up a woman behind the counter who looked to be about Sid's age. She had long, wavy hair the color of dark rust, big expressive eyes so blue, Sid could see them from several feet away, and her smile was easy and open. Her dress was very much bohemian, with a lovely blue-and-cream pattern that suited both the woman and the shop.

She spied Sid and smiled, but then let Sidney browse in peace, which she appreciated. There was nothing worse than a hovering salesperson. The women finalized their purchases while Sidney ran her hands over the display of throws. She settled on steel-blue Egyptian weave and grabbed a couple of vials of essential oils as well as a diffuser.

The woman introduced herself as Poppy while ringing up her order.

"Are you new to town or just visiting?" Poppy asked with a smile as she ran Sid's credit card through the machine. "It's hard to tell these days. The town is growing so fast, and with all the development on the other side of the lake, we've got a lot of new folks here for the long haul."

"I'm here for a vacation, I guess." Sid hadn't thought about what it was exactly she was doing in Crystal Lake, other than getting away from where she'd been.

"Well, there's lots to do. Still snow on the ski hills, if that's your thing."

"Actually, I'm just looking to relax and disappear."

Poppy looked up, and for a second, there was something in her eyes that made Sid wary.

"It's a good place to do that," Poppy replied softly. She handed Sid her bag. "Where are you staying? At the new resort?"

"No. I'm renting a place. A beautiful stone cottage on the lake. Nate Jacobs is a friend of mine, so he hooked me up."

"Right. I heard Beck was renting out the cottage."

Beck. Sid had to work hard not to roll her eyes, but then something loosened her tongue.

"So you know Nate and his brother?" she asked casually.

Poppy laughed. "Sure do. Nate and I are the same age, we were in school together from kindergarten right up to graduating high school." She smiled. "And Beck, he's older by a few years, so he was the hot guy who seemed so unattainable. But then through most of high school he and Cate were joined at the hip, so it's not like anyone had a chance with him anyway."

That piqued Sid's interest. "Who's Cate?"

Poppy's eyes clouded, and her smile slowly faded. She

fiddled with a small ceramic cardinal, and for a moment, Sidney thought she wouldn't answer. "She was Beck's fiancée."

Was?

The doorbell tinkled, and they both looked over as a young mother and child walked in, effectively cutting off their conversation.

"Do you know of a good place to grab lunch?" Sid asked as she backed away with her purchases. She decided she needed food before tackling groceries.

"Depends on what you're looking for. There are a couple of new places downtown that serve higher-end sort of stuff. Or you can go across the lake to the resort. There're a few places there. The Blue Elephant is one."

"I'm thinking more along the lines of the best burger in town." Her stomach rumbled at the thought. "And maybe some onion rings." Sid couldn't remember the last time she'd had anything but salad with chicken or fish for lunch.

"Well, for that you'll have to head out to the Coach House. It's just over the bridge and past the mill."

"Thank you." Sid headed back to her SUV and less than five minutes later was parked at the Coach House. The building looked like an old barn, as if it had been around for generations, which gave it a certain sort of charm she appreciated. There were a lot of vehicles in the lot, and, though it took a few moments for her eyes to adjust, once she was inside, she noted most of the tables were full.

A young woman greeted her with a smile and led her to a booth. She introduced herself as Kaia, presented the specials of the day, a turkey clubhouse with tomato soup and garden salad, and then handed Sid a menu.

"You can keep that. I know what I want." Sid flashed a smile. "I want a cheeseburger with the works and an order of onion rings and a water please."

"You got it." The girl hesitated for a moment. "This is going to sound weird and stuff, but you look real familiar."

"Do I?" Sid replied lightly.

Kaia nodded. "Anyone ever tell you that you look like Sidney Barrett? Do you know who she is? She knows everything about everything. Just last week, I used this recipe she had up on her website, like a homemade paste to detoxify your skin, and I swear it made all the difference in the world. I follow her on the Gram. You should too. Lots of tips about pretty much everything. She's, like, perfect."

"Far from it," Sid muttered.

"What was that?"

"Make sure I have pickles with my burger, please."

"Sure. No problem."

Sid watched Kaia walk away, and it was then that she caught sight of a group of men sitting at a high table up near the bar. Three were looking her way, while the fourth read over the menu. It was the fourth who caught her attention. One of the others knocked him in the arm and said something to make him laugh. He suddenly looked up, their eyes met, and for the life of her, she couldn't look away.

She wanted to. Badly. But couldn't.

He was so...direct and unwavering. And for a brief moment, his smile stayed in place, changing everything. Beck Jacobs wasn't just devastatingly handsome, he was beautiful. When his smile faded, she tried to look away, but that damn invisible tether held them fast.

Sid was aware of voices and music, and she nodded absently when Kaia approached with a tall glass of water, finally able to tear her gaze from Beck's as she accepted it and drank half in one gulp.

She realized her heart was beating rapidly and exhaled, pointedly avoiding looking in his direction while she waited for her food. What was it about him that knocked her on her ass like this? She grabbed her phone from her purse and scrolled through the many messages that sat there because she needed something to do in order to effectively ignore the man.

There were three from her sister threatening a visit if she didn't answer soon.

Two from her business manager with questions about some of the content she'd filmed for social media and her website in advance of her escape. She made a mental note to call him back.

One from her landscaper to let her know he'd been at her place and would be back in five days to aerate the lawn.

There were several messages from various companies she worked with, and a few from companies who wanted her to use their products. She made a note to forward those to her business manager.

It was the last message that stole her breath and sank her heart.

Nick.

Her eyes blurred at the sight of his name and the heart emoji still attached to it. She didn't open the message for a few reasons, the main one because she couldn't see. Sid pushed the phone away and stared at it blindly, jumping when Kaia appeared with a plate of onion rings and her burger.

Her appetite was gone, but she accepted the food and nibbled at a few onion rings. The wave of sadness hit like it always did, pretty much paralyzing her, numbing her to everything else. She didn't see the folks around her chatting and laughing as they caught up over a plate of wings or a basket of fries. She didn't see looks sent her way by those very folks, probably seeing her as the stranger she was and wondering where she'd come from.

She didn't see Beck slide off his stool as the men finished up their lunch and headed for the exit, while he stood there and looked her way as if contemplating something. And she certainly didn't see him hand Kaia his bill and some cash before heading in her direction. Sid only became aware of him when he slid into the booth and sat across from her.

She glanced up, surprised, and found herself caught by dark eyes that saw too much. Quickly, she turned over her phone and took a few seconds to compose herself before looking his way again.

"Don't take this the wrong way, but you're probably the last person I want to spend lunch with," she said lightly, meeting his gaze.

"After last night, I don't blame you one bit." He didn't hesitate, and his eyes never wavered from hers. "It's kind of why I'm here."

"Oh?"

"I want to apologize, if you'll let me."

"Do I have a choice?"

"Nope." He cracked a smile, but she didn't reciprocate.

"I was a dick, and—"

"You were obnoxious and rude and arrogant as hell."

"I was going to say rude, but I guess obnoxious and arrogant are good too." He had the nerve to look contrite, just when Sid was getting riled up again remembering his behavior. "Look, I don't have an excuse other than to say..." His eyes darkened, and his voice trailed off. For a moment, she thought she saw something familiar in him, and it made her heart skip. But then he looked away, and the moment was gone. "Actually, there is no excuse and there's nothing I can say, so I hope you accept my apology and we can start over."

"You're lucky I'm not the type to hold grudges."

He sat back, obviously not leaving, so she felt the need to offer up some conversation. "How's the kitten?"

"I dropped it off at the clinic this morning for Molly to look over and assess."

"So you're keeping it?"

"For now, I guess. I was hoping someone could foster the damn thing, but apparently, there's no one available. It looks like he'll be with me for a few more weeks until they can adopt him out."

"Well, the good news is that cats are independent creatures. I'm sure the little guy won't be too much trouble."

"Yeah?" Beck got to his feet. "How do you know that?"

Sid blinked a host of memories away. "I used to have one."

Beck stared down at her for a couple of seconds and then took a step back. "I've got to get back at it. Enjoy your burger."

Sidney watched him leave, noting how almost everyone in the place said goodbye or acknowledged him in some way. He was well liked from what she gathered, so she assumed his behavior the night before wasn't the norm. She saw the way their eyes lingered on him, as if there were more to his story than what little she'd glimpsed. Then she thought of what Poppy had shared. Of Cate, a fiancée from the past.

And then she thought that maybe...

Maybe he's like me.

CHAPTER FIVE

By the time Beck finished up at the bungalow, it was dark. He took one last look around the kitchen, his critical eye noting a few things to add to his to-do list. In a couple more weeks, the place would be ready to sell. He'd bought it from the bank when they'd repossessed the property over a year ago, and it had been an ongoing project. He'd knocked down walls, opened up the floor plan, and taken most everything else down to the studs.

The place looked nothing like its former self, and he felt pride as he took in all his hard work.

He'd make a tidy profit, no doubt about that.

His cell pinged just as he was locking up, and he pulled it from his pocket. It was a text message from Molly. The kitten was a healthy little girl, approximately eight weeks old, and she was dropping it off at his place on her way home.

Great. Some part of him had hoped she'd have found a foster family for it, or taken pity on him and brought the kitten back to her place. With a sigh, Beck pocketed his cell and hopped into his truck. It was Monday night, which meant hockey with the boys, and he was looking forward to blowing off some steam. He stopped at the coffee shop downtown and grabbed a ham sandwich before joining his brother and a few other guys, including Nash Booker and Hudson Blackwell in their dressing room.

He got into his gear and shook his head in amazement at how much things had changed in only a couple of years. No longer was the room full of trash talk and bravado. Now it was Blackwell asking Booker how the baby was. Or Jack Johnson wondering what kind of diaper he should be buying for his son because the ones his wife picked up didn't do the trick. Then his brother piped in about Molly and her mood swings, wondering how best to handle them.

"First thing I learned." Hudson laughed at that. "Just say yes to anything she wants."

Beck was out after that. He grabbed his stick and headed for the ice, content to play the game and burn off the dark energy that seemed to have settled over him for days now. Afterward, he headed back to the Coach House for wings and beer. The guys were riding a high after beating their rivals, the Ice Kings, and he nursed a mug of ale while waiting for the food. Nathan surprised all of them by joining the team at the bar; he usually headed home to Molly as soon as the game was over. He slid on to the stool beside Beck and grabbed a mug from Hudson.

"Good game," Nate said. "You were on fire."

Beck grunted an answer. He'd scored four of their six goals.

Hudson held up his mug. "The Rust Buckets just might make the playoffs."

They all cheered at that, as it had been a few years, and Beck settled back in his seat.

"Look, I don't want to get up in your business, but I feel I should warn you." Nathan took a sip of beer and glanced at his brother. "Mom will probably be popping by at some point."

"She was at my place this morning before you were out of bed."

"Man." Nate shook his head. "She's fast."

"Yeah." Beck leaned back and shrugged. "Don't worry about it. I was an asshole last night, and she wanted me to know that she knew. I told her not to worry about me, and I apologized to your friend."

"Sid?"

"Is there another friend of yours I need to apologize to?"

"Are you always so damn sarcastic?"

"No." Beck grinned. "Only with you." He paused. "We're good. I know you guys mean well, but like I told Mom, I'm fine. I'm hoping that now you and Moll and Mom know to back off when it comes to my private life."

Nate held up his hands. "You don't have to worry about me. I'm done with all that matchmaking crap."

"Good."

The boys settled in and, as usual, tall tales were told, gossip was swapped, and before he knew it, a couple of hours had passed. Beck was still nursing the same beer he started out with, so he pushed it aside, tossed some cash down, and said his goodbyes.

"Where're you off to in such a rush?" Nash Booker grinned from across the table. "It's early."

"It's been a long day." That nervous energy was back, and Beck gave one last wave before heading out into the cold night air. He stood at the bottom of the steps for a few seconds, his breath making smoke rings as he exhaled, and then scooped his cell phone out of his pocket. He searched through the numbers and sent a message.

You still up?

A few moments later, he saw the three dots signaling a reply and waited.

You coming over?

Was thinking about it

I'll be in the hot tub

Beck read the messages over a few more times, hand on his phone, because he was torn. He didn't want to be that guy. The kind who used women for sex and nothing else. Though, to be honest, this thing he and Emily had was equal parts usage on both sides. They'd gone into this with an understanding, and as long as that understanding wasn't challenged, the status quo was good for both of them.

He was on edge and riding close to something that couldn't be good. There was only one way to get rid of it. It was time to scratch that itch.

Be there in five

He sent his reply and headed to his truck, pointing it in the opposite direction of his place when he left the Coach House. It didn't take long to cruise to the other side of town and pull up in the driveway of a cute little bungalow he'd worked on a few years back. It was set way back from the road, which was why he didn't mind coming out here. And with no neighbors to the left and old Mrs. Crump on the right, so far the rumor mill hadn't picked on whatever it was he had going on with Emily Davenport.

The door opened under his hand, and the soft glow of candles threw shadows everywhere. He stepped out of his boots and grabbed the cold beer waiting for him on the kitchen island. He took a few swigs before walking over to the garden doors that led out back. He stood there for a while, enjoying the silence, and glanced to his right at the photo that sat on a small table.

It was a candid shot of Emily and her husband, Rick. A big guy with a big heart and an even bigger laugh, he and Beck had been friends since they were kids. Five years ago, Rick had taken his motorcycle for a spin and missed one of the bends on River Road. His injuries were severe, and he'd been in a vegetative state ever since. Currently, Rick was a patient in a specialized wing at the hospital, where he'd been since not long after his accident.

Emily loved her husband. Of that there was no doubt. And this thing between them? It was only physical. It's why it worked for him.

Beck pushed open the doors and walked onto the back deck. The yard was private and dark, with several candles set on the table to his right, and to his left was the hot tub.

"That was fast," Emily Davenport said softly.

"I was at the Coach House."

"Hockey?"

"Yeah."

She moved closer to him, rising above the edge of the hot tub until her breasts were visible. The ends of Emily's long blonde hair were damp and clung to her skin, and as the night air met her heated flesh, her nipples pebbled.

"You coming in?" She sank back into the steaming water.

Beck finished his beer, got undressed, and tossed his clothes on the table. He slid into the hot water and sank back, instantly feeling some of that tension leave him. The two of them sat in the hot tub for several minutes without speaking, or touching, or anything really. They stared up into the midnight sky and let the silence wrap them up in the kind of comfort they gave each other. A familiarity born from pain, and an understanding no one else they knew had.

"How's the house coming along?" Emily moved closer, her big blue eyes half-lidded from the heat and the half-empty bottle of wine on the side of the tub.

"I should finish soon," he said, watching her closely.

"Did you have a good Christmas?"

"It was the same as always."

"I hear ya there. Sometimes I feel like nothing is ever going to change." She reached for her wineglass, but it was empty.

Instead of filling it up, she moved toward Beck and straddled him.

"I've missed you. It's been a while."

"I've been busy."

She held his gaze for several seconds. "Yeah. I know." Her mouth slid over his, and before long, he was inside her. This wasn't making love. There were no long, tender moments. This was about fulfilling a need. A need that changed from time to time. Sometimes, it was about not being alone. Other times, like tonight, it was about the kind of release he could only get through sex.

They had no label for what they were doing, but it had worked for four years. Yet tonight, something was off. And it bothered Beck, because he couldn't put his finger on it. As he stepped out of the hot tub, she sank back into the water.

"Aren't you going to stay?" It was something he usually did, though he was up and out of her bed before dawn.

Beck reached for his clothes and pulled on his shirt. He shook his head. "I've got a kitten to get back to."

"A what?"

He heard her surprise.

"I found a kitten in my truck, and she's little, so I need to get back to her."

He wasn't sure if Emily believed him or not, but she didn't say anything. Didn't throw a fit or start a fight. Another reason this worked. She never questioned anything, and neither did he.

Once he was dressed, Beck paused, that off-kilter feeling still banging around inside him. "You okay?" he asked quietly, turning back to her.

She shrugged, that sad smile he'd grown used to in place. "I'm never okay, but it's something I've learned to live with. Same as you." She reached for the wine bottle and topped up her glass. "You sure you don't want to stay?"

Something in her voice got to him, and he paused. "Do you need me to?"

The jets kicked in, and she sighed, sinking deeper into the water. "No. I'm being silly. It's the wine. Go home to your kitty, Beck. I'll see you around." She closed her eyes, and he headed out, closing the door quietly behind him.

He was usually relaxed when he left Emily's place—for obvious reasons. But tonight was different. Tonight, he felt out of sorts. Lately, it seemed as if nothing could fill up that hole inside him. Not even a little bit.

Beck decided to do what he always did in this type of situation. He pushed it to the back of his mind, tucked it away in a corner he had no desire to visit, and headed home.

CHAPTER SIX

By Thursday, Sid had read five books, one of which consisted of over seven hundred pages, an impressive feat by anyone's standards. She'd learned a few new yoga poses, gone to the spa across the lake for a facial and massage, caught up on *The Bachelor* and three of the *Housewives* reality shows, and was now bored out of her mind.

If this was what relaxing was all about, she needed to up the game. Her staff had been instructed not to contact her unless her business was burning down, and so far, she'd heard not a peep. Not even from Kylie, and that had to be some kind of record.

She'd just had lunch on the back deck in the sun, and the view was lovely. After all that cold and snow when she'd first arrived, the temps had soared, and she only needed a light jacket to keep warm. The steady drip of melting ice off the roof nearly lulled her to sleep, but she hopped up, cleared away the remains of her toasted tomato sandwich, which was mainly crumbs and the end of a pickle, and decided to go for a walk and enjoy this first taste of spring. She grabbed her cell phone and a pair of sunglasses and locked up the place.

When she got to the end of the driveway, she crossed the road and found the trail that ran perpendicular to the road and the river, which made it easy for Sid to know where she was at. The air was fresh, the sun warm, and she spied squirrels darting among the bushes, as well as robins and blue jays swooping overhead. Buds were beginning to sprout on the bare-limbed trees, though there were plenty of evergreens for color.

By the time she spied Manchester House, she'd been hiking well over an hour, and when she noticed Molly's SUV in the driveway, she crossed the road. Maybe she needed some human interaction after all.

Sid was about to head up to the house when she heard Molly's voice coming from the outbuilding, which she understood to be an animal shelter of some sort. She changed course and, since the door was open, walked inside with a hesitant "Hello." Molly was bent over a table, back facing Sid, and turned at the sound of her voice.

"Hey," she said with a big smile. "This is a nice surprise."

"I hope I'm not bothering you."

"God, no. Actually, I could use a little help. I just took delivery of these little guys, and an extra hand to feed would be great."

Sid walked over to the table to find a litter of puppies, six in total, in a basket. They ranged in color from light tan to near black, and one was completely white. They were adorable and incredibly small and fragile.

"How old?"

"Between two and three weeks. Their eyes are just beginning to open."

"What happened to their mother?"

Molly fetched six syringes full of formula and handed one to Sid. "I have no idea. They were dropped at the clinic in town overnight. Lainey, the lady who runs the office, found them this morning when she went in to work. My brother dropped them off about thirty minutes ago. I've got a foster mom coming to grab them, but they need to be fed now." She handed Sid the white puppy.

Sid cradled the little guy or girl, she didn't know which, and, after a few attempts, was able to feed the puppy successfully. She fed two more and was just placing the last one back in the basket when an older lady walked into the shelter. Her faded red hair was piled high on her head, and an easy smile lit up her face when she spied Sid and Molly. She wore a colorful coat of pink and red and purple, and baby-blue pants tucked into black rubber boots. The epitome of eccentric, she greeted Molly warmly.

"Sid, this is Serena Fairbanks. She's one of my best fosters." Molly paused. "Her daughter owns this cool boutique down along the river."

"Bella something or other?" Sid asked, eyes on Serena.

The woman nodded and smiled. "You've met my Poppy."

"I have. Her boutique is lovely."

Serena was silent for a few seconds, her gaze intense as she studied Sid. "I feel like I know you." Sid didn't get a chance to respond because she saw the *ah-ha moment* light up the woman's face. "You're Sidney Barrett. I love your show and your website. So much great information. I watch it all the time." Her face scrunched up. "I just... You were on TV last night."

"I was." Sidney nodded. "I taped a bunch of segments before I left so that we'd have content."

"Good to know." Serena winked. "Why, I can't believe you're here in our little corner of the world. How long are you staying?"

"I don't know," Sidney admitted. "I haven't had a vacation in forever, and I needed a break. Nate's a friend, and he convinced me to come to Crystal Lake. He said it would be good for my soul, and he's right." Sidney blinked and thought about that. Nate was right. She was more relaxed than she'd been in a very, very long time.

"Well, I hope to see you again." Serena peered into the basket, her smile faltering. "Who on earth would leave these puppies overnight? We're damn lucky a coyote didn't get them, or a raccoon."

"I know," Molly sighed. "At least our mystery owners did drop them off instead of..."

"Instead of what?" Sid frowned.

Molly turned to her and shrugged. "Some folks around have been known to tie up a litter of kittens or puppies in a garbage bag with rocks and toss it into the lake."

Sidney's mouth dropped open in horror. "That's awful."

"It is. It's not as common as it used to be, so we're making headway. Over the last decade or so, we've got more shelters in the area, and I think in general, folks are more educated. They get their pets spayed and neutered. And for those that don't, we have lovely people like Serena to help us out."

"Speaking of which, I should get these babies back to my place and settled so they can snuggle in and sleep, the poor little things."

Molly slid from her stool and braced her back with a grimace.

"Are you all right?" Concerned, Sid took a step closer.

"Oh, I'm good. It's just the babies." She made a face. "I mean, aside from the stretch marks and heartburn, ankles the size of a small child, and boobs so big I can barely get them tied down, I probably wouldn't even feel pregnant."

Sid attempted a smile, hell, she was probably even successful. But her face felt frozen, and it took a lot to move her mind along from things best left in the past.

She took the bag of formula and supplies from Molly. "I'll

walk these out with Serena. Why don't you head inside, and I'll come in and make some tea, unless you want a nap? I can always head back."

"Tea sounds great."

Once the puppies were packed up in Serena's old Chevy, Sid got busy in the kitchen. Molly allowed herself one cup of tea a day, and the two of them enjoyed it together, seated by the large bay window that overlooked the backyard and lake.

"I don't think I'll ever get tired of this view," Molly said, shifting into a more comfortable position.

"It's beautiful here. I can't believe I waited until now to visit this part of the country."

"You've never been this far north?"

"I've been to Canada and Alaska, and I go to New York City several times a year, but I've never stepped foot in Michigan until now. The first time I met Nathan, he told me I was wired too tight and if I needed to shed all that stress, a visit here would do the trick."

Molly turned from the window. "How are you doing?" Her tone was gentle. "I mean, you don't need to answer that if you don't want to. I just...I don't know specifics of your situation, but I do know that Nate was worried about you when you first called him." She shrugged. "He has good instincts."

"I'm good," Sid replied after a few moments, more than a little surprised to realize just how good she felt. "I had some stuff happen. Personal stuff that blindsided me, and I didn't handle it well. I was headed to a dark place, and I think my sister was scared for me. She was the one who called Nate, and then he got in touch, and one thing led to another, and here I am." She tried to keep her voice light, but she wasn't sure she'd been able to keep that pain from her words.

"Life sucks sometimes," Molly said. "But whatever it was you went through, it's obviously made you stronger."

"I think so. I don't feel as low as I was, and it was pretty damn low. But it's also made me reevaluate things. And sometimes that's more confusing than the initial event or problem. If that makes sense?"

"Yeah. It does." Molly set down her teacup. "I'm glad you're here and that this place, all this nature and the lake and the people here, can help you get to where you want to be." She made a face. "I'm just sorry my brother-in-law nearly ruined it. I don't know what got into him. He's not usually such an ass."

Sid picked at an invisible piece of lint on her tights. Heat crept up her neck, and she averted her eyes. "He can't be all that bad. I ran into him the other day, and he apologized. In my books that means we're good."

"I'm glad to hear it. I haven't seen him since the night you arrived. And honestly, he really is a good guy, you know? He just..." She sighed, and Sid glanced up at Molly. "He's had some awful things happen, and like a lot of guys, he bottles stuff up. When he lets it out, it's not always pretty."

Curious, Sid hesitated, but then couldn't help herself. "What's his story? I've heard something about a fiancée. Poppy mentioned it, but she didn't elaborate, and I didn't ask. Didn't feel it was my place. Nate's never shared anything about his brother to me."

Sid thought she might have overstepped, because for the longest time, Molly was silent, but then she sat back and smiled, a sad sort of thing.

"Beck and Cate were, like, the perfect couple. In high school, everyone wanted to be them. He was tall, athletic, really good-looking, and she was...perfect. Always smiling, so nice and funny and talented. She was an artist, and we all thought she'd go places. They dated all through high school and college, and a week after graduation, they got engaged. No one was surprised, though I think Beck's parents and Cate's hoped the engagement would be a long one, since they were so young." Her voice trailed off, and Sid noticed tears shimmering in the corners of Molly's eyes.

"One Saturday morning, on a day a lot like this one, she was jogging along River Road when a drunk driver coming back from some party across the lake hit her. They didn't find her until hours later, when Beck started freaking out because she never showed at his place. The guy that hit her, a local, Dave Matthews, left her in the ditch, and she was gone when they found her."

Sid's throat was tight, and she felt answering tears poke her own eyes. "That's awful," she whispered.

"It was. She was so young and had so much potential. Cate was the love of Beck's life, and he was the same to her. He's never been with anyone else. I mean, he's moved on and he's living, he is a human, and, like all of us, he has needs, but he doesn't date. And I worry about him. He's an amazing man, and someone would be damn lucky to belong to him, but he's not interested."

"He loved her that much," Sid said. She understood because she knew what it was like to love someone so much, the world ended when they left.

"He did, but..."

"But what?"

Molly sighed. "They were so young. Who knows how things would have turned out? I just...I don't feel this is all there is for him, but nothing I say makes a difference."

"His heart isn't ready," Sid said softly.

"I guess not." Molly glanced at the clock. "Holy cow. It's nearly five, and Nate should be home soon with pizza. You'll stay?"

"Oh no. I should get back. I don't want to intrude."

"Not taking no for an answer. Poppy's supposed to come by

as well. I haven't seen her in ages, so help yourself to a glass of wine, and I can inhale the scent and pretend I'm having one with you."

Sidney got up and did just that. Why not, she thought. It wasn't as if there was anything or anyone calling her back to the stone cottage. Besides, she'd been alone for days now, and it felt good to be around Molly.

She'd just poured herself a generous glass when she heard the front door open and Molly's dog, Petal, came bounding through the kitchen, claws scraping across the wood floors as she struggled to keep her footing on legs too long to navigate properly. The gold-and-white dog spied Sidney, and it took everything in her to keep from spilling the wine when Petal came at her, tongue flopping in excitement, tail wagging like crazy. The dog barked up at her, and she couldn't help but smile at the animal's pure joy.

"Hey," she said with a chuckle. "Calm down, girlie."

"I'm afraid the word calm isn't in this particular dog's vocabulary." The accent was English, and the deep voice belonged to a tall man with broad shoulders, striking blue eyes, and a devilish grin that could make a nun's panties fall off with one look. He gave her a long, slow perusal and winked, walking over to her with his hand out. "I'm Link."

"I know."

She knew exactly who he was, which wasn't surprising since he was one of the most famous men on the planet. As the number-one-ranked footballer in Europe, if not the world, he'd come out of nowhere and over the last few years had been featured in magazines and campaigns for high-end products the world over. Sid didn't have to be a soccer fan to know who he was. He was on the same level as Beckham or Cristiano Ronaldo, men whose good looks and charm contributed to a fame that transcended both the sport that made them famous and the country they were born in.

His wicked grin deepened. "Is that a good thing or a bad thing?"

"It just a statement of fact," she replied with smile, taking his hand. "I'm just wondering what you're doing here is all. I mean, I'm going to assume you're one of Nate's clients, but shouldn't you be playing somewhere?"

"I should, yes, but I'm not." His words were clipped, and though the smile didn't leave his face, his eyes had hardened. Sid knew there was more to the story, but he wasn't sharing, and it wasn't any of her business anyway.

"I stayed in Crystal Lake a while back and kind of fell in love with the place. I rented this house, actually, until Nate, the bastard, bought it out from under me."

"Don't be bitter, Link. The place you bought is better suited for you." Molly was on her feet and shuffled over for a hug. "Is that my husband I hear?"

"He's right behind me."

Just then, Nate strode into the kitchen with two large pizzas, and just behind him, Beck. The sight of him made Sid's stomach flip, and that damn heat was back, fingering its way up her neck. Her heart leapt into her throat when he smiled at his brother, because, man, what a smile, and then he turned, catching sight of her for the first time. He didn't look away, though his smile slowly faded. Was it displeasure? Or surprise.

"Hey," he said, walking past to set down another brown bag of takeaway on the counter.

"Hi." She sipped from her wine because she needed something to do. She all but forgot about Link until he spoke, his voice so close, she almost jumped.

"Is the pretty lady staying for pizza?"

"Of course she is," Molly said, leaning into Nathan.

Sid looked at Beck and found his eyes still on her. They were dark and unreadable. Not exactly friendly, but at least he wasn't spitting nails either. In fact, there was something about them that tugged at something inside her.

"I'll stay if Beck brought his manners along," she replied slowly.

"I don't know about my manners," he said with a wry grin in place. "But I promise to try to be good." The smile changed everything about him, and Sidney took another gulp of wine because her reaction to him was that strong.

"What's the fun in that, mate?" Link chuckled. He glanced between the two of them, then narrowed his eyes. "Bloody hell, good luck with that."

Bloody hell is right, Sid thought, tearing her eyes from Beck. There was something here. She felt it in her bones. But was it one-sided? And if not, what did that mean? Based on his past and what she'd just learned, the smart thing to do would be to run as far away and as fast as she could, put as much distance between her and Beck Jacobs as humanly possible.

Maybe Sid was done with the running thing. Or maybe she was just curious to see if and where whatever this was would go. And to be curious meant that part of her wasn't as dead as she thought. That was a good thing, right?

CHAPTER SEVEN

Beck wasn't planning on staying long. Hell, he hadn't planned on staying for dinner; he'd given the boys a ride back from town after Nate's truck died and was towed to the garage. It had already been a crazy week, and he had a full day of work scheduled for Friday. His plan was to finish up the bungalow by day's end and fit in a couple of appointments he had with his Realtor to look at a few properties he was considering for his next project. With a buyer already in hand for his current one, he was eager to find something else to work on.

They'd just finished eating. He and Link insisted on cleaning the kitchen while the girls relaxed in the living room and Nate took Petal out back. He stacked the last dish in the dishwasher and rolled his shoulders, eyes on the girls as they giggled about something. Poppy and Sid were having an animated discussion about the Kardashians and pop culture, while Molly looked content to put up her feet and listen.

"I'd ask which one you've got your eyes on, but it's pretty obvious." Link cracked open a beer and leaned against the counter.

"You don't know shit," Beck replied, shaking his head. The Brit was always looking to stir the pot. Not for the first time, he wondered when the hell the guy was headed back to Europe to play soccer.

"I know enough," he said. "Trust me."

Beck didn't bother to respond. Instead, he folded the pizza boxes into the recycling bin and ignored the man.

"Of course, if you don't lay claim, then that means it's open pickings for me."

"You sound like a dick. Even for a guy."

The man had a reputation, that was for sure. And there'd been several women from town who'd thought to catch him, but so far, the Brit had proved elusive.

"I wouldn't get too excited." Beck chuckled. "Poppy knows better, and you're not Sid's type."

"You know her that well, do ya? This Sidney from San Diego with her creamy skin and all that long, dark hair."

Beck frowned. From what he'd observed, the footballer had a thing for Poppy. His eyes were never far from her, and he'd been more than eager to sit beside her at dinner. Good luck with that. Poppy Fairbanks was a bit of a mystery to most of the men in town. She didn't date, and she sure as hell didn't let anyone touch. At least according to locker room talk, which Beck knew not to take too much stock in. Guys were worse than women when it came to gossip.

Poppy was a nice girl, but she was also aloof. According to his brother, who knew her better than Beck did, she'd gone to LA straight out of high school and had come back a different person.

Nate walked in just then, Petal hot on his heels, and looked at the men. "Anyone up for a game of pool?"

"Not me," Beck said. "I've got a big day tomorrow, so I'm up early, and then there's that damn kitten. She can't be left alone for too long. I'm even running home at noon to give her some attention, which is ridiculous."

"Yeah? Why's that?" Molly was in the kitchen now, hand on the small of her back, and good Lord, but her belly was huge.

"I came home the other day, and the drapes that hang in the front window were in a pile on the floor, and she'd knocked over my coffee cup, which had coffee in it, and that was a sticky mess, and she played in her litter box, and that crap was everywhere, including the sticky mess of coffee."

"Have you named her yet?" Sidney asked. She and Poppy had followed Molly into the kitchen, and they stood a few feet away.

Beck made a face. "Jingle."

"What was that, mate?" Link laughed.

"Jingle. Her damn collar has balls on it that jingle when she runs around, which is a lot. Kept me up for hours last night. I think she's the spawn of Satan. She can't be normal."

"It's called a kitten," Molly replied. "And that's totally normal."

"Whatever she is, I need to get back to her while my house is still standing."

"You done with the bungalow?" Molly asked.

"I should be tomorrow. I'm looking at a place down by the park and then the old church by the river."

"I thought it was condemned."

"It's in rough shape, but I'm thinking it could be interesting. It's on a good-sized lot, two acres at least."

Molly looked confused. "What would you do with it?"

"I'd make it into a home." Up until now, he hadn't really thought about it, but the idea took root, and excitement bloomed in his chest.

"Does it have stained glass?" Sid asked, taking a step closer.

He nodded. "It was built in the 1800s. All brick, with large stained-glass windows and the kind of workmanship that's hard to come by these days."

"Why is it empty?"

"I think folks stopped going to church, and they couldn't afford to keep it with such low numbers, so they just closed up."

"That's sad," Sidney murmured. "A place built in love and faith to just be abandoned like that."

Beck wasn't a particularly religious man, but he saw her point.

"I did a series of videos on old churches in the South a few years back," she said. "The detail and architecture on a lot of them was impressive, and the stories of the people they belonged to were incredibly inspiring."

"Videos?" Link asked. "What is it exactly that you do?"

Beck noted the surprise on her cheeks and the way she averted her gaze. The woman didn't like calling attention to herself. Which was odd considering her job. He'd googled her a few days back and had been surprised himself to see that Sidney Barrett was a bona fide celebrity in her field. An up-and-coming Martha Stewart. It added another layer to the woman that made her more interesting.

"I have a lifestyle show and website," she said. "As well as every social media platform you can think of."

Link winked. "So you're on the telly."

"I am."

"I'll follow you on Instagram if you follow me."

I'll think about it," she replied wryly.

"You should take Sid to see the church," Molly said. There was an awkward pause as Link, Sid and Beck looked her way. "I mean, if she wants to go see it."

Beck was happy to give Sid an out, considering she'd been put on the spot. "I'm sure Sid has better things to do other than poke around old abandoned churches."

"Actually, I'd love to see it."

It probably should have surprised Beck that the thought of sharing his work and this church in particular should feel good, but he didn't dwell on it too much. "It's an early trip. I'm meeting Olivia at seven thirty, so I'll be heading out shortly after seven."

"I'll be ready." Her answer was light, though she didn't quite meet his gaze. He wasn't sure what that meant, but since Beck wasn't the best at reading signals on a good day, right now he was tired and decided it was best not to overthink.

"Okay." Beck took a step back. "I should go. Thanks for the pizza, bro. I'll see you Saturday."

"What's happening on Saturday?" Molly asked, clearly puzzled.

Nate dropped a kiss to her nose. "Our hockey tournament and the dinner and dance."

"Oh. Right." She chuckled. "Pregnancy brain."

"Yeah, well, don't feel bad. It's spreading."

"What's that supposed to mean?" Molly teased lightly.

"I just got a text from the garage. Nothing catastrophic took down my truck. It was, ah, out of gas."

"Takes balls to admit something like that." Beck laughed. He said his goodbyes and headed back to his place. When he got there, he cut the engine and stared up at the dark house for a few moments. The house was nothing to look at it; in fact, it held no warm fuzzies for him either. It was just a place to hang his hat and hold the bed that he slept in.

He thought about the church and the plans inside his head. And he wondered...maybe this would be the one that finally felt like home? Bah, he thought. The Manchester place was supposed to be the one. Hell, he used to brag to Cate that he'd buy it for her. When he finally finished the house, after working on it for nearly three years, he'd walked out, and if not for his brother buying it, he'd probably never have gone back.

Not used to feeling so damn melancholy, he yanked on the door handle and slipped from the truck. He'd barely made it inside when almost immediately, a ball of purring, meowing, and shaking fur hit him in the leg and began to claw his ankles.

"Hey, there," he said, scooping up Jingle. The little girl rubbed her head and cheeks against him, almost aggressively, and began to knead his chest with her tiny paws. She looked up at him, those green eyes of hers wide, that little mouth and those whiskers shaking as she meowed over and over again. "Geez. I haven't been gone that long."

She meowed, a long and plaintive wail, and the hairs on the back of his neck stood on end.

"Hey, I gotcha."

He held her close to him as he stepped out of his boots and checked on her food and water. Both of them were in good order, and he gave her a scratch behind the ears. "At least you only emptied half the litter box on the floor today. That's an improvement."

He carried on to his bedroom and put her on the bed before hopping in the shower. Ten minutes later, he was stretched out on the mattress, the bundle of fur purring madly on his chest, and as Beck stared into the darkness, something stirred inside him. Some kind of feeling he hadn't had in a long, long time.

As if she knew something had just shifted, Jingle meowed and burrowed as close to him as she could. It was no use locking her in the mudroom because all she did was meow her damn head off, and he'd already been through too many sleepless nights since she arrived.

Beck closed his eyes, the purring machine next to him, and thought the guys would razz him good if they could see him. But really, he didn't give a damn. In fact, his mind was on other things, because along with that mysterious feeling that hung in there, tight in his chest, was the thought that it would be nice to have someone here with him from time to time. In his bed. Tucked into his side. Maybe even there in the morning when the sun came up.

The weird thing being, it wasn't Emily's face he saw when he closed his eyes.

The eyes that watched him from the shadows, the body curled into his, belonged to Sidney Barrett.

It was an image that stayed with him until he drifted off.

CHAPTER EIGHT

Sid was up early, at least an hour before the sun rose. By six thirty, she'd showered and dressed, taken some time with her hair and makeup, and had already had two cups of coffee before heading outside to fill the bird feeder out front. By seven, she was nearly jumping out of her skin. Too much caffeine, she told herself. What else could it be?

She glanced at the mirror, at the flushed cheeks, subtle makeup, and shiny hair, and wondered if she was trying too hard. Then she asked herself, trying too hard to do what? Impress Beck? Nah.

"He's not interested," she murmured. But then she thought about his dark eyes and the way they made her feel whenever they landed on her. And of that smile of his. It was like a secret weapon, one he didn't use often from what she could tell, but man, when he did...

Her cell rang just then, and she gave herself one last look and grabbed her phone from her bag without thinking or looking to see who was calling. She was still a little rattled at the direction of her thoughts. Still unsure. And definitely worked up about something.

"Hey," she said distractedly, rummaging in her bag for her sunglasses.

At first, there was nothing, and then everything inside her stilled. The hair rose on the back of her neck, and her stomach, already full of butterflies, flipped over, and she felt nauseous.

"Hey," he said. "It's me."

Sidney closed her eyes and sank against the counter. His voice was intimate, as if he were standing next to her. She didn't answer at first because she couldn't. And somewhere deep inside her soul, a part of her was pissed that this was her reaction to him. That after months of no contact, months of Sidney trying to forget and move on, of trying to push away the anger and betrayal, he could call her up and say hello as if nothing had happened.

"Sid?"

"What do you want, Nick?" She found her voice at about the same time she found her balls. "And how did you get this number?"

"It's barely seven where you are. Kind of early to be pissed off at the world, isn't it?" His tone was neutral, and he was treading lightly. "I just..." He paused. "I was thinking of you. I wanted to check in, and I thought we could talk."

"You don't get to think about me. Or wonder. Or anything. You're a lying bastard and that doesn't come close to being the shittiest thing I can say to you."

"Say what you need to. I can take it. I need to fix things."

She so didn't need this from him. He was about six months too late. But honestly, this anger was so much better than the hurt and pain. At least with anger burning through her veins, she felt alive. And that sure as hell was a welcome feeling.

"What makes you think I want to talk to you about anything? I thought I was pretty clear on things the last time we spoke."

"You know I'm sorry for that."

"Those are just words." Tears poked at her eyes. "You never showed, Nick." The words tumbled out of her, and she inhaled a ragged breath. "I was there alone, and you never showed. On top of everything else, that is one thing I will never be able to forgive you for. That was it for me. I told you then I never wanted to see you or talk to you again, so I repeat. Who the hell gave you my new cell number? I'm assuming it's one of my staff, and I need to know who it is so that I can fire them ASAP."

"I don't want to get anyone in trouble. I just wanted to make sure you're okay."

Fury.

Red. Hot. Fury.

It knifed through her, sharp and invasive and so strong, her voice shook along with her body.

"You don't have the right to ask if I'm okay. Or wonder what I'm doing, or where I am or who I'm with, doing all those things you're wondering about. And trust me," she nodded as if he were standing right in front of her, "I'm doing things. *Lots of things.* You gave up that right when you left me there alone, when you betrayed everything we had. Then you made me doubt myself. You told me it was all my fault. That your actions were a direct result of all that noise you said I created. You took zero responsibility and made me feel like shit. You didn't just break my heart and my trust, you threw it away with no regard and showed me what a selfish bastard you are." Her voice grew louder as that fury and anger emboldened her. She was having a moment. A beautiful, glorious moment of recognition, of ownership.

For the first time in forever, Sid felt as if she wasn't a passenger in this wreck of a life she'd found herself in, but, in fact, she was driving the train and about to run over the thing standing in front of her. The thing preventing her from moving forward.

Nick Sanchez. Former fiancé. Former cheating bastard. Former breaker of her heart.

"You don't deserve what I have to give. You never did. And I'm just realizing that now."

She was done feeling sorry for herself. Done with living in the past and dwelling on a future that would never come because someone else decided to throw it away. So what if she only had half a heart? It was more than some folks had.

In that moment, she realized it wasn't losing Nick that had sent her spiraling. It was the other thing she'd lost. And that ache would never go away.

"Come on. Don't be mad. There was a lot of good too. I know you're holed up in Michigan. I have business in New York City. I'm here until Sunday. I thought that...I was hoping maybe to visit. I..."

"Nick," she interrupted. "I'm going to say this one last time, and I really need you to pay attention. Okay. Sit down and listen." She paused. "Are you listening?"

"Yeah." He sounded unsure. "I'm here."

"Go. *Fuck.* Yourself."

She tossed her cell back into her purse, then threw her hands in the air and did a victory dance. God, she felt free and light and...

Beck stood by the front door, watching her. "Oh," she said, breathing a little heavier than she'd like.

"I knocked," he said, obviously uncomfortable. "But, ah, you didn't answer, and I heard raised voices, and the door was unlocked, and I thought..." He shrugged. "I don't know what I thought, but I should have waited for you to answer. I'm sorry. I didn't mean to barge in."

Sid shook a long strand of hair from her face, grabbed her

jacket and purse and walked toward Beck. "It's all good. I was just taking care of something I should have taken care of a long time ago." She breezed past him and didn't stop until she got to his truck.

"I locked up for you," Beck said, sliding behind the wheel. "Okay," he said, glancing her way. "Let's do this."

Sid was silent as they headed to the town proper of Crystal Lake. It was easy to sit back and not say anything, on account of the fact the wind had left her sails and she was wondering what exactly Beck had heard. Plus, the radio was on, some local morning show by the sounds of it, and the host was going on and on about ice fishing.

They drove down Main Street and across the bridge and, once on the other side of town, hung a right just past the river, where the homes were large, with equally large tree-lined lots. After a few minutes, the homes came fewer and farther between, and eventually, they came to a fork in the road. Beck continued along the right, onto what looked more like a laneway than anything else, and at the end of it, up on a knoll that overlooked the river, sat a beautiful stone church. Some of the gorgeous windows were broken, most likely from rocks thrown by kids, and the steeple leaned a bit to the right, but the bones of it, the very meat of it, was intact, and Sid stared at it in wonder.

"It's beautiful." She turned to Beck with a big smile. "It's so much more than I expected, and I haven't even seen the inside yet." She peered to the left of it. "Is that an old graveyard?"

He nodded. "Some of the oldest settlers in the area are buried there."

"You don't..." She looked back at Beck. "Does it come with the church?"

"No. It was separated from the church a long time ago. I believe it's heritage land now."

A car pulled in behind them, a sleek silver BMW. Beck got

out of the truck, and Sidney followed suit, though at first, the woman in the car didn't see her. She was chatting away to Beck, long blonde hair stirring in the breeze, expertly applied makeup on point, complete with plump glossy lips and perfectly lined brows. She was dressed in a smart camel duster, with a cream sweater underneath, and tan slacks tucked into knee-high brown boots. The woman was put together. Sid assumed she was the Realtor.

She stood a little too close to Beck for a professional meeting, at least in Sid's mind, but maybe out here, they did things differently. The woman leaned closer and giggled.

Nope. She was on the hunt for more than just a sale.

Her hand was on Beck's arm when Sid walked up to them and held out her hand.

"Hi. I'm Sid."

The blonde slowly removed her hand from Beck and shook Sidney's. "Olivia." She glanced up at Beck. "I didn't know you were bringing a friend."

"We're not really friends," Sid said. "We just met."

"Right. Okay." Olivia cleared her throat. "Let's go have a look, then, shall we?"

Sid followed Beck and Olivia inside, and from the moment she stepped foot inside the church, she was filled with wonder. She left Beck and Olivia and walked around the entire church herself. From the main worship room to the alcove off the back, then up to the loft. Tucked away in the far corner was a door that led to a small library filled with dusty old books, a quill and dried-up ink bottle, as well as paper with words long faded. A smaller window let in a lot of natural light. When she peeked out, it was the river she saw.

She walked back out to the loft and stared down at the space still full of pews, carved long ago from trees taken from the nearby forests. There were a few wall hangings, maybe silk?

And her mind started to turn as she thought of where to send them to be refurbished and of plans to open the place up into a home. How best to incorporate all the elements here, to save this sliver of time and place and worship and make it into something spectacular.

The design of the pulpit was simple and standard, not too big and not too small, but the wood was solid oak with hand-carved words running the length of it. Scriptures from the looks of it. She'd never seen anything like it before. She walked back down to the main level just as Olivia and Beck came out of the small alcove.

The woman said something soft and low to Beck before giving Sid what Sid called the professional smile. Sidney knew it well because she used it all the time. It looked open and warm and inviting, but didn't quite reach the eyes. It was a smile saved for business acquaintances, or folks you interacted with in a non personal way. Or those you didn't care all that much for.

When the Realtor left, Sid turned to Beck, who stood there holding the keys in his hand, eyes on the loft overhead.

"You're going to take it, aren't you?" she asked, walking over to where he stood.

"It's a big project."

"It's amazing," she replied, turning in a full circle. "God, I'd make a great room over here, with a huge kitchen and family room. That area over there could be a guest room or two, and a bath. The alcove could be an office, and the loft would be an amazing master bedroom, with a huge walk-in closet, bathroom, and there's the cutest library up there."

Beck smiled at her. "You're more enthusiastic than Olivia."

"Well, that's because Olivia was looking to sell something other than the house."

"Yeah?" Beck looked surprised at her comment. "And what was that?"

She stared at him, kind of shocked, but not really. The man honestly didn't know the effect he had on women. Or if he did, he chose to overlook it or ignore it altogether.

"Never mind," she replied with a smile. "Thanks for bringing me out here." She turned in a full circle again. "I really liked this. How long have you been doing this? Flipping houses?"

"I kind of fell into it, I suppose."

"It happens. I sorta fell into my line of work too."

"And how does one fall into being famous?"

She blushed. First off, she hated it when people called her famous. Her face was recognizable, yes, but she was no Aniston or Jolie. She didn't have to hire security or hide from the paps, and she could still be anonymous if she wanted to.

"It just happened," she said. "I started posting things on Instagram that I liked, food and makeup and books I enjoyed. All kinds of stuff. And it kind of blossomed from there."

"I enjoy working my hands," Beck admitted. "And after I decided to stay in Crystal Lake, I started working as a carpenter, which is still my main gig. But I found I needed more projects to fill my time and bought a wreck of a house that turned a tidy profit. I reinvested that profit into the next one, and things kind of snowballed."

"Well, the stone cottage is amazing, so I'm not surprised."

He held up a set of keys.

"These belong to the house I'm considering as an investment. Olivia had to meet up with another client, so she gave them to me. I'm heading there next. You want to tag along, or do you need to get back to the cottage?"

She followed him back outside, though she paused to take one last look around. "I'd love to come."

She spent the next hour looking over an average two-story that was in quite the state of disrepair, which they discussed thoroughly when Beck insisted on taking her out for breakfast. They stopped at a small place in the downtown core, and the owner, a Mr. Barton, knew Beck well.

"It feels like everyone knows everyone in this town," she said when they were done.

"It's both a curse and a blessing, I guess."

They were headed back to the lake and her stone cottage, and Sid found herself wishing she had the rest of the afternoon to spend with him.

"Did you ever consider leaving?"

And just like that, the atmosphere changed. His lips thinned, his eyes darkened, and his voice was flat. "I had plans once. Had my sights set on different things. But my reason for leaving left, and I stayed."

Sidney didn't know what to say to that, so she kept quiet. When they got back to her place, she pasted a smile to her face and slipped out of the truck. "Thank you. I really enjoyed today."

"Yeah." He smiled at her, but it was no different from the smile Olivia had given her in the church. It didn't reach his eyes. Clearly, his mind was on other things. "I'll see you around."

She stepped to the side as he backed out of her driveway, and as she walked toward the stone cottage, she noticed for the first time that the sun had disappeared. It kind of fit her mood. She made a face as she reached for the door, but then felt something on her cheek.

It was snowing again.

CHAPTER NINE

Beck worked his butt off Friday afternoon in order to finish painting the last bit of trim so he could call this particular project officially done. He left the bungalow just after six and went to the arena to play game one of their tournament, which they won. From there he stopped by the Coach House for wings and a beer because he was famished.

And because the guys wouldn't take no for an answer.

He didn't stay long because he knew Saturday involved at least three hockey games and, if they made the finals, the last game of the season. After the week he'd had, he knew he needed a good night's sleep on account of the fact his legs weren't getting any younger and there'd be a lot of skating the next day. When the hell did getting old become a thing? He didn't like it one bit.

He ignored a message from Emily, which he felt bad about. He told himself he had no energy for a tumble in the sheets, but there was more to it than he cared to admit. He'd stared at her name for a few moments and then tucked his cell back into his pocket. He'd gone home and fallen into bed, exhausted.

Saturday was dull, with a cloud-heavy sky, which a lot of

folks found disappointing after the warmer temperatures they'd enjoyed the last few days. Not that Beck or any of the guys he knew cared. They spent the whole of it at the arena, doing what Michigan boys did. They played three games of hockey and, after making the finals, managed to bring home the win. They were champions of the Monday Night Men's League.

The dressing room was full of the kind of camaraderie only a close-knit team full of childhood friends could produce. The atmosphere was light, there were a lot of laughs, jokes, most of them off-color, and some horseplay. The guys looked forward to the party at the community center, which was conveniently attached to the arena. Wives and girlfriends came, a band was set up, the beer would flow, and it was catered by the Coach House, so there'd be lots of fried goods, as well as burgers and dogs.

What more could a guy ask for?

Up until now, Beck would have said *nothing*. Not a damn thing. But he'd been off for days now, and he had no idea why.

"You okay?" Nate asked, sitting down beside Beck to pull on his boots. Both of them were fresh out of the shower.

"I'm good." Beck pulled on his black Henley and reached for his black leather jacket.

"You seem quiet is all."

"I'm just tired." Beck tossed Nate his tweed coat. "You ever regret coming back here?" Shit. Where the hell had that come from?

"What do you mean?" Nate frowned and slipped into his coat.

What *did* he mean? Beck shrugged and shoved his hands into the pockets of his jeans. "You were all set up in a life in the city, and now you're back. And this place...sometimes it's a lot. A guy can't give himself a scratch without someone seeing."

"Don't I know it." Nate fiddled with the buttons on his coat.

"My life took a left turn the day I injured my knee and my hockey career ended before it began. I knew then all bets were off and that I'd have to rethink things. But did I see myself back here?" He shook his head. "Nope. I liked New York City. I made a life there. I loved my job, and things were good. But then Molly happened, and now I can't picture myself anywhere else. She's a townie for life, and wherever she lays her head is where I need to be." Nate narrowed his eyes. "What's this about?"

"Nothing. I just... It's been a weird week."

"Do you regret staying? I know you had plans, that you talked about going to San Francisco with Cate and then..." Nate looked away.

"Yeah." Beck ran his hands through his damp hair and sighed. "No, I don't regret staying in Michigan. I mean, I don't think so. It's just sometimes I feel like I'm standing still. And then there's Mom. I don't know what it would be like not to have her poking her nose in my business."

"You could move to Timbuktu and she'd still find a way to know what's going on. There's no place on earth where that's a reality."

"What the hell, boys. This conversation is sounding way too philosophical." Randy Armstrong threw his arms around both of them. "What say we go and get us some beer and have a couple of laughs without the women breathing down our necks?"

Nate chuckled. "Well, my woman is waiting for me, hopefully with a cold beer in hand, but hey, you do you buddy." It was common knowledge among the men on the team that Randy Armstrong was a bit of a horn dog, especially when he was liquored up. His wife knew it too, and if Beck were a betting man, he'd lay down a crisp Benjamin and say that Sheila Armstrong was waiting for her husband outside the dressing room to keep him in line.

Beck followed his brother out to the arena lobby, nodded a

quick hello to Sheila, and spied Molly at about the same time he noticed Sidney standing beside her. He stopped in his tracks, surprised to see her. In small-town America, she stood out, and he couldn't put his finger on why. It wasn't as if she was outrageous or anything, and there were plenty of attractive women in town. She wore a pink jacket over a plain tan shirt, paired with faded jeans that fit like a glove, tucked into brown leather boots. Her outfit was simple and classy, and her hair tumbled down her back in loose waves.

She turned, and they locked eyes, and damned if the world didn't tilt just a little bit. The feeling took Beck by surprise, and he frowned, unsure how to respond. He took a step forward, intent on making his way over, when long, delicate fingers closed around his forearm and stopped him.

Emily.

"Hey," she said with a warm smile. "Great game, and congrats on the championship. You guys must be pumped."

He nodded and mumbled an affirmative. He might have said something about the weather. Who the hell knew?

"Is your phone dead or something?"

"What?" Distracted, he turned to her, his tone sharper than it should have been.

Her eyes narrowed a bit, then shadowed with what seemed like hurt, and that made Beck feel like shit. She let go of his arm.

"I just meant that I was thinking about you last night. I messaged, but you didn't respond. It's not like you."

"Em, I'm sorry. I was beat and was home and in bed by eleven."

"No worries." Her tone was light. "I came to watch the finals. You played against Rick's team."

"Right." This was awkward, no way around it. And for the life of him, Beck didn't know why. Usually things between him and Emily were easy. They were friends with the secret benefits, but friends first.

"It was a good game."

Beck nodded his thanks, turning slightly to find Sidney's eyes still on him.

"Who's that?" Emily took a step closer and followed his gaze.

"With Moll? That's a friend of Nate's."

"She's definitely not a townie." There was no snark in Emily's words; it was just an observation.

"No."

"Where's she from?"

Beck dragged his gaze from Sid. "San Diego, I believe."

For a moment, Emily didn't say anything. She lowered her lashes, and he couldn't get a read. "You seem to know an awful lot about her."

Shit. Here we go.

"Not really. I just met her last weekend."

Emily looked over their way and then back to him. "She's stunning."

"She's attractive," he admitted, because he'd have to have a hole in his head not to notice just how beautiful Sidney was.

The set of Emily's mouth told him he'd just said the wrong thing. He didn't want to do this. Not now. Not ever. He had a feeling he and Emily had just crossed a line he never intended to cross, and it was probably time to take a look at things, because she was acting like he'd done something wrong.

"I should go," she said lightly, taking a step back from him. "Will I see you later?"

Beck held her gaze a heartbeat longer and then cleared his throat. "I don't think so. It will probably be a late night."

"Oh." The reply was soft. Resigned. "I figured." A sad smile touched her generous mouth. "I'll see you around." She turned and disappeared through the crowd, taking the back exit that led to the parking lot.

Beck wasn't exactly sure what had just happened, but he felt like crap about it. He didn't want to hurt Emily. And even though he knew she was just looking for a body to lie next to, a connection she'd lost the day her husband crashed his bike, he couldn't be that person anymore. He couldn't fake something he didn't feel.

He turned and walked over to his brother, Molly, and Sid, who'd now been joined by his parents. Warmth bloomed in his chest. He was a few years past thirty, and it still mattered when his parents came to watch him play.

"Good game, son." Beck took the praise his father offered and shook his hand. He was good, no doubt about that, but his brother had been a pro. Even with a weak knee, Nate could skate circles around every single guy in the league. And then some.

"Was that Emily Davenport?" his mother asked, looking over his shoulder.

"Yeah."

"How is she? I haven't seen her at the hospital in a while. Though I suppose it's because they moved her husband to that new wing. Such a shame. Melinda, Rick's mother, said they're hopeful he'll wake up one day and Ethan Caldwell is convinced he will too, but..." Her voice trailed off for a few seconds. "I don't think Ethan has ever forgiven himself for heading out with Rick that day."

Beck nodded. Ethan had been...was...Rick's best friend. They'd grown up like brothers, and he'd been MIA since the accident. Kept to himself and showed his face in town when he had to.

What the hell could he say to that?

"I was just telling Nate's friend Sidney about the church

you're thinking of buying, and she told me she's already seen it." His mother smiled. "I don't know what I have to do to get an invitation to see it, but clearly, being your mother isn't enough."

Her voice was light and teasing, but he heard the questions. He knew his mother. She was wondering how they'd gotten from Beck being rude and acting like a dick, to Sidney coming along to see the church. He gave her hug and kissed the top of her head. His mom could wonder all she wanted, because he sure as hell wasn't going to offer an explanation.

He wasn't even sure what that explanation would be.

"Don't worry about it, Ma. I'll take you over whenever you want. Though I haven't decided yet on whether to buy it or not. It's an ambitious project and a huge commitment."

"I think it's one of the most amazing structures I've ever seen, and the possibilities are endless." Sidney glanced at him. "I hope you decide to purchase it."

Samuel Jacobs tugged on his wife's arm. "We should go and let these kids have fun."

The four of them watched his parents leave, and then Nate grabbed his wife's hand. "I need beer."

"I need food," Molly replied with a giggle. "Let's go."

Beck fell in place beside Sidney as they followed his brother and wife into the community center. It was already crowded, but the champions had a long table reserved, conveniently located near the bar and to the left of the stage.

"Are you a fan of hockey?" he asked Sidney as they maneuvered through the crowd.

"This was my first game. It was exciting. Really fast," she said, waiting for a couple of guys to move out of their way. "I'm West Coast, though, so I'm more of a baseball kind of girl."

"Padres?"

"Giants all the way."

"Huh."

Sidney stopped cold and looked at him. "What's that supposed to mean?"

"What?"

"You said, 'Huh.'" Her right eyebrow arched.

"It's not supposed to mean anything. I'm just surprised you're not a fan of the team that calls your city home. San Francisco is a bit of a hike to watch a game."

"Well, Mr. Jacobs, I'm going to go out on a limb and say that there's a lot about me you don't know."

"I think I know plenty," he replied, hiding a grin. They stood a few feet from his teammates gathered around the table, and as he looked down into Sid's eyes, the noise in the room faded. In the low lighting, her features shone like a beacon, and he had to wonder... Had her lashes always been so damn long? Had her lips always been full and soft like a pillow?

That thought made him pause. Did he just compare her lips to a pillow? What guy did that?

"Do you now," she replied, a hint of a smile touching those lips he was trying to forget. Gone was the fatigue that had plagued him most of the week. Hell, it was only twenty-four hours earlier he was dead on his feet. And now he felt as if could go back onto the ice and skate at least a hundred laps of the rink.

It was one hell of a second wind.

"I do," he said.

"Then share." Sidney was clearly enjoying herself, and damned if he wasn't as well.

"You're left-handed, like a good number of artistic folks, and you're nearsighted."

"How did you..." She looked puzzled. Or impressed.

"You squint when you're looking at something far away." He paused and cocked his head. "You have a high metabolism and can pretty much eat whatever you want." When she opened her mouth to say something, his grin widened. "I've seen you eat, remember? It's an impressive thing. You also dislike onions."

"You saw me pick them off the pizza the other night."

"I did." He rocked back on his heels and then leaned closer. "You like red wine, but I'm going to say you're not averse to the occasional beer. You like to read, watch movies that make you cry and," he glanced over to the bar, "with the selection on hand, you're going to order up Bud Light."

Sidney's mouth fell open, and he had to work hard to resist the urge to close it. *With a kiss.*

Jesus. He took a step back. What the hell?

"You're good," she said after a couple of seconds, her surprise evident. "How did you know I like sad movies?"

"That part I guessed." He was jostled from behind. Armstrong had been drunk since noon and now crashed into Beck's back. Pushed forward, he nearly took out Sid. He grabbed her by the waist in order to keep himself upright, and an electric pulse hit him square in the chest. He let go of her like he'd been holding a hotcake.

"Do you want a drink?" Beck moved back a few paces. Lord knows he needed some space.

Her gaze settled on him, and her eyes seemed to glitter through the darkness. Beck found himself holding his breath.

"You seem to know everything," Sid said lightly, and her tongue darted out to touch the edge of her mouth. They stared at each other a heartbeat longer. Then her smile widened. "You tell me."

CHAPTER TEN

Sid almost bailed on the hockey game.

She'd been in a weird melancholy mood since the day before and was pretty sure Beck Jacobs had something to do with it. Or maybe everything. She'd spent the afternoon working on some new ideas for her brand, and when Molly called her up and asked her come to the championship game with her, she'd initially refused. She'd given Molly a lame excuse, told her she was tired and was going to spend the night with a good book and a bottle of wine.

But an hour or so later, after staring at the same two pages of her book until her eyes blurred, she sat back and thought about the church Beck had taken her to and how amazing it would look with all the plans in her head. Then she thought about Beck and the sadness in his eyes. Which led to thoughts about his smile, that rare bit of ease that lit up his face and turned him from handsome to devastatingly hot.

She'd stared down at the book again, wondered about him and this hockey game and if he'd be celebrating with everyone afterward—according to Molly, it was tradition to go to the dance party. Then she tossed the damn book, called Molly, and told her she was in.

Now she stood a few feet behind him as he sidled up to the bar with his brother to get them drinks, and was trying not to stare at his butt. She lowered her eyes and couldn't help herself, but in her defense, it was one hell of a fine-looking ass.

"Hockey butt."

"What?" Startled, she looked up at Molly, who was grinning like a cat who'd just caught the proverbial mouse.

"Look around. They all have them. Hockey butts. It's from years of skating." Molly pointed to Beck and Nate. "Those tushies are pretty much the cream of the crop, but still..." She made a comical face. "They're everywhere. It's like butt heaven in Crystal Lake." Her grin widened. "One of the many perks of living in a small hockey town in Michigan."

Sid giggled. "You guys would be smart to include that in the town's travel and tourist brochures."

Molly winked. "Who says we don't?"

"Don't what?" Beck handed Sid a Bud Light and took a drink from his own, a questioning look on his face.

"Nothing," Molly replied, slipping her arm into Nate's as she leaned into him. "My back is killing me, babe. Can we sit?"

"Sure thing." Nate dropped a kiss onto her nose. "Let me know when you've had enough. I'm good to go home anytime."

Their love and attraction, the softness in his eyes when he looked at her, was enviable, and Sid glanced away as an ache bloomed inside her. What that ache was, exactly, was up for debate. Was she lonely? For sure. Was it more than that? Probably. Where did Beck figure into things?

The fact that he'd even entered her mind should have freaked her out, but instead, she turned to Beck and found him watching her intently. No longer were things light. No longer was their earlier, mild flirtation in play. This was different.

There was something definitely going on here, and Sid actually played around with the idea of seeing where it went. Would it be so wrong to explore whatever this was? She was a grown-ass woman, after all. And sure she had baggage aplenty, but so did Beck.

"We'll grab some seats, guys." Molly tugged on Nate's arm and dragged him toward the table.

"Can I get an introduction?" The newcomer who appeared at Beck's side was a bear of a man. He had a couple inches on Beck (who had to be at least six foot three, so the man was huge), and his shoulders were as wide as a truck. His head was bald, with some kind of tattoo inked on the side of it, his jaw and chin shadowed with hair, and his eyes were so dark, they appeared black. He was dressed in red plaid flannel and jeans, and his boots were untied.

He looked at Beck and frowned. "You in la-la land or what?"

Before Beck had a chance to answer him, he turned to Sid and offered his hand. "I'm Ike McBride."

Her small hand disappeared inside his, but she couldn't help but smile up at him. She decided he was a gentle giant and immediately liked him.

"I'm Sidney, but everyone calls me Sid."

"Well, Sid, since Beck seems to have forgotten how to speak, it sure is nice to meet you."

"I haven't forgotten how to speak, McBride. It's just hard to get a word in with you sometimes." Beck gave the man a quick hug, the kind that guys do, complete with the quick pat on the shoulder.

Ike grinned. "True."

Another man appeared beside the giant. "I gotta steal this one for a group photo before half the team gets too liquored." The guy winced. "Armstrong is already there."

"Go on," Ike said. "I'll look after your friend."

"I'm sure you will," Beck replied dryly before turning to Sid. "I've got to do this thing."

"Go. I'll be fine."

She watched Beck walk over to a bunch of guys, including Nate. A couple of them clowned around, but when the man who'd fetched Beck got out his camera, all joking disappeared. Someone set the trophy in the center, up front, and they lined up like pros.

"We take our hockey seriously in these parts." Ike grinned. "Even beer league." He lifted his chin toward the group of men. "Those bastards have made it to the finals for the last four years. And that was before Nate joined up last fall. They'll probably be winners until Nate quits."

"I see that," she murmured, eyes on Beck as he put his arm around his brother. The two of them chatted about something, and when he smiled at Nate, it damn near took her breath away.

"So, Sid, where you from?"

Ike's voice drew her away from Beck, and she took another sip from her can. "San Diego."

"And you're in Crystal Lake because..."

"I'm renting a stone cottage on the lake. Nate is a friend and hooked me up. I was looking to get away from things for a bit." She grimaced. That was simplifying things. She'd been drowning for weeks.

"This is certainly more laid-back than the city, that's for sure."

"Right?" She flashed a smile. "I was born in Los Angeles, and we moved to San Diego when I was four, so the city has always been my home. This here? This cute small-town life, it's different."

"I hope in a good way."

She nodded and was surprised at how much she liked it here. "For sure. There aren't too many people I still talk to that I knew when I was a kid. It's strange to me that the majority of all these people have known each other all their lives. Take Nate and Molly. They grew up together. And Beck, I mean, do you guys go back as well?"

Ike slowly nodded, but his smile dimmed a bit. "I've got a few years on those boys, but I've known Beck since he was a skinny teenager, with shoulders too wide and legs too long for his hundred-and-fifty-pound frame." He paused. "He used to date my sister, Cate."

"Cate," she repeated softly. "I'm so sorry. I...I've heard about your sister."

"Thanks." Ike finished his beer and crushed the can. "She was good stuff." He glanced up. "They were good stuff together."

Sidney didn't know what to say to that, so she nodded and said nothing. She wondered about Cate. About a woman who could inspire such love and devotion so long after she'd passed. Was there ever a woman as fierce as that alive?

Ike tossed his beer into a large trash can to his left. "I should go. It was nice meeting you, Sid." He gazed past her. "It's good to see Jacobs out socializing. The guy works too much." He winked. "I hope to run into you again."

Sidney said goodbye and made her way over to the table. She was restless and didn't feel like sitting, and when the band started up, she and Beck watched from the shadows, sipping their Bud Lights, enjoying the music and, surprisingly, each other.

Nate and Molly stayed about an hour and offered them a lift home, but Beck had just bought another round of beer, and Sid decided to stay.

"Right," Molly said. "You guys can share a cab."

"You should call now and schedule it for later because Pete the cab guy will be busy." Nate shook his head. "Last week, I waited nearly forty-five minutes after our game for a ride home."

"You only have one cab guy in Crystal Lake?" Sidney couldn't keep the shock from her face.

Beck nodded. "On this side of the lake, anyway."

Nate pulled Molly away, and they disappeared while Beck sent a text to Pete the cab guy. "He'll be here at midnight."

"Okay," she replied, voice a little too soft and a tad too husky.

The air was thick between them. Thick with something that had her skin buzzing as if an electric field covered her whole. As if her skin was alive, infused with something, some spark she'd forgotten existed.

Desire.

Beck smiled down at her, and her heart leapt. Her lady parts sang. Her breath hitched. She knew he felt the same way because she'd caught the long looks and hooded gaze. They didn't acknowledge it, but instead, settled into an intimate corner to watch the band. Maybe they were invisible, or maybe they gave off some kind of aura, because no one bothered them. They were able to just be, to exist beside each other on a night she'd not seen coming.

It had been ages since Sid felt anything like what was happening inside her. She wasn't dead inside after all. And she supposed that was a good thing. That after all this time, after Nick's betrayal and the trauma afterward, she was alive. Sure, it was a damaged version of the person she used to be, but heck, life damaged everyone, so what was wrong with that?

When the band slowed things down and pulled out a moody Eagles song from their repertoire, the dance floor filled with couples. She stood beside Beck and watched, heart still beating faster than it should, breath still falling in short, quick spurts.

Beck swayed a bit, and she realized he'd probably had a lot to drink. A lot more than she had, anyway. According to Molly, the guys had been playing since noon, and most of the men were well on their way to hangover Sunday.

"You like the Eagles." He tossed his empty beer into the bin.

She eyed him warily. "I do."

"This song in particular is one of your favorites." A slow grin curved his mouth, and her knees went to jelly. She'd like to say it was from the booze, but that would be a lie.

"It is." God, he was good.

"You want to do something about it?" His eyes were a bit glassy, and she knew he was definitely on the drunk side. But did she care? His grin deepened. Hell no.

"I didn't take you for the kind of guy who likes to dance in public."

Beck reached for her, and she literally stopped breathing. He leaned close and angled his head so his mouth was near her ear. His breath was warm on her skin, and she shivered. "Seems like you don't know me as well as I know you."

He led her to the dance floor and slipped his arms around her, though he held her lightly and didn't pull too close, even though she wouldn't have minded that one bit.

They swayed together slowly, while the band's rendition of *Love Will Keep Us Alive* washed over the entire room. He didn't say a word, and neither did she. Instead, her fingers splayed across his chest, and what they touched was hard and warm. An image of him that first day they'd met, when the only thing he'd worn was a plaid shirt he'd not bothered to button up, flashed in her mind's eye, and she rested her cheek against his shoulder, letting him take control and lead.

He smelled damn good, a mixture of male and something fresh, most likely from the shower. She closed her eyes as that ache came back with a ferocity that left her weak-kneed and out of breath. When was the last time a man had held her like this?

It was Nick, of course, but even before the end of Sid and Nick, they hadn't had whatever it was she felt right now. Intimacy in the middle of a crowd was a heady thing, and when the song finally ended, she was left stunned at the depth of need inside her.

I want him. Which should have surprised her, but kinda didn't.

But does he want me?

Beck's cell pinged, and he let her go so he could search through his pockets for his phone. He took a look and stared at it for a few seconds.

"Pete's here."

"Who?" she managed to say through lips suddenly so dry, she could taste sawdust.

"Pete the cab guy."

"Oh." Sidney took a step back. This was it. The night was over. "Yes, we should go, then."

Beck nodded and, with his hand at the small of her back, lightly guided her out of the community center. He said goodbye to a few of the guys, but most of them were still caught up in the celebrating thing and didn't notice him leaving.

It was brisk outside, and the snow that had begun the day before continued leaving several inches in its wake. By the time she slid inside the cab, she was glad for the heat. Beck climbed in beside her and sat back, hidden by the shadows. Sid settled in the seat, shivering a bit from the cold, or maybe from all the zigs and zags shooting off inside her.

He made small talk with Pete on the drive out to the lake. The cab driver asked about the bungalow he was working on, said that his sister was looking for a house to buy, and Beck told him to give her his information and he'd make sure his sister got a look before it hit the market if she was interested.

"I'll do that," Pete replied, taking a left onto River Road.

The rest of the trip was silent, but that was okay. She needed some time to get her shit together, because right now, she felt like her fifteen-year-old self, and that wasn't a good thing. Fifteen-year-old Sid had been all over the place.

They pulled into Beck's driveway, and for a moment, she froze, unsure where things were headed. Mixed signals had a way of screwing with one's head.

"Do you want to come in?" he asked after a few moments, his voice warm and husky.

"I'm not sure that's a good idea," she managed to reply.

"I wasn't asking if it was a good idea or not. I was asking if you'd like to come inside."

Heart pounding so loud, she was pretty sure Pete the cab driver could hear, she licked her lips and melted at the look in Beck's eyes when they fell to her mouth. "Since you know me so well, what's my answer?"

Praise Mary and hallelujah. She could still speak.

He stared at her for a heartbeat or two—actually, it was more likely three and felt like ten—and then that slow smile she was getting way too use to crept over his face.

"I think your answer is, damn right I do." He handed Pete some cash and hopped out of the car and waited for her.

She couldn't move, and he peered inside.

"Unless, for the first time tonight, I'm wrong."

Do it.

She gave Pete a quick, awkward wave and followed Beck, her feet crunching over the cold, hard snow. When he unlocked the door to let them inside, she resisted the urge turn her butt around and run for the hills. Or the lake. Or the forest. Or whatever was out there. Instead, she got her shit together and followed him in.

Almost immediately, a meowing bundle of fur hurled itself at Beck. He scooped up the little kitten while shucking his boots. A lamp was on, but the place was pretty dark.

"Can I use the bathroom?" she squeaked in a voice that would make her fifteen-year-old-self cringe.

Beck pointed toward a hallway. "First door on your left." He held up the kitten. "I'll just look after this little girl, and then..." He grinned, and she all but ran to the bathroom.

Once inside, she whipped out her cell and called her sister. It was just about six in the evening on the West Coast, and Kylie picked up on the first ring.

"I met someone," she whispered hoarsely, watching the door as if it were alive and eavesdropping.

"What?"

"I met someone." She spoke a little louder and winced at the sound of her voice in the quiet.

"Oh my God. Details."

"I'm in his bathroom."

Silence. Big loud silence.

"You met someone, and you're calling me from his bathroom?"

"Yes."

"Are you drunk?'

"Kind of."

"Is he hot?"

"Like lava."

Her sister chuckled. "Then why are you in his bathroom?"

She felt silly. And scared. And anxious. And...

"I don't know if I should be here. I don't know if I'm ready, and he's, you know, he has stuff like I do." Sid swore and played with the end of her hair, twirling it into a tight string.

"Everyone has stuff, trust me. You should do this. Now get your butt out of the bathroom and get naked with this mystery man, and then call me tomorrow, because I want to know everything. And Sid?"

"Yes?"

"This is a good thing. If you made it as far as his bathroom, then you can get the rest of the way to his bedroom and have some hot, mind-blowing sex. You'll thank me tomorrow."

Kylie hung up on her, and Sid pocketed her cell before pinching her cheeks and applying a touch of gloss to her lips. She washed her hands, tousled her hair, and marched her butt out of the bathroom, only to find Beck nowhere.

She stood in the dark for a bit and then tiptoed back down the hall. Since there was only one door open, she peeked inside. On the bed, stretched out in a pair of jeans and nothing else, was Beck, with the little kitten curled up on his chest. The kitten was purring up a storm while Beck was sound asleep.

They looked adorable. She let out a long breath and scooped the blanket from the end of the bed. She pulled it over him, taking a swipe from the kitten's paw as the little minx asserted her ownership.

"You can have him for now," she whispered softly. She eyed the other side of the bed, but Beck was sprawled out on his back, smack dab in the middle. She knew he'd had an intense workweek, then all the hockey today, and with the booze added in, it must have taken its toll.

She headed back out to the living room, found another old knitted throw on the edge of an ancient-looking sofa, and curled up on her side. Not exactly the night she'd envisioned, but for some reason, she was okay with it.

At least for now.

CHAPTER ELEVEN

Beck woke up to sunshine streaming through his window, which told him he was already behind. He groaned. God, he ached in places he didn't think possible, and realized he just might be getting too old for a weekend full of hockey. Everything protested—his arms, his legs, his abs—and he rolled over, face-planted into a pillow, and stayed that way until an annoying little paw made it impossible.

He turned his head and found Jingle one inch away, staring at him intently.

"You hungry?" he asked, rolling off the bed. He stretched his arms over his head and grimaced before heading to the bathroom to take care of business. A few minutes later, still barefoot and shirtless, he padded out to the kitchen, Jingle hot on his heels. The little girl meowed up a storm until he filled her food dish, then she turned into a purring, vibrating ball of fur.

He stared down at her and shook his head. Who knew this kitten would worm her way into his life so completely? And in a week, no less.

He rubbed at the scruff on his face and eyed the coffee

machine. Was a pot enough to shake the fog from his head? He'd come home and passed out like an amateur. But the hours of work, coupled with four hockey games in one day and more than his fair share of beer, had a lot to do with it. At least that was the story he was sticking with.

No doubt about it, he was getting older, and it sucked.

He took exactly two steps into the kitchen and stopped cold. *Sidney.* He turned and stared across the room at the front door, a frown marring his forehead. She was with him last night. She'd come *here* last night after he'd practically dared her to. And then he'd...

He'd fallen asleep on his bed waiting for her to come to him. What an idiot.

"Jesus," he muttered, and walked to the living room.

Her boots were at the front door, so she was still here. He found her curled up on the old sofa he'd taken from a house he'd demoed a while back, a ratty old throw his grandmother had given him wrapped around her real good. He couldn't see her face—her long dark hair was a mess of waves that covered most of it—but a delicate hand was wedged underneath her chin, and the edge of her nose poked out from all that hair.

She was out cold, and, not wanting to disturb her, he headed back to the kitchen as quietly as he could. He made a pot of coffee and, while it was brewing, had a peek in the fridge. He was a pretty good cook, but from the looks of things, he was currently running low on supplies. He had three eggs, a milk carton with a questionable date—but hell, it passed the sniff test—two slices of cheese, half an onion, a slightly shriveled green pepper, and one bagel.

He could work with this.

In no time, he whipped the eggs and milk together and then let them cook over medium-low heat while he chopped up some pepper and onion. He layered that overtop of the eggs, then added the cheese slices on top, grabbed the bagel, which he sliced in two.

His toaster was shot, so he grabbed another pan to grill the bagel, just as Jingle meowed loudly and he turned his head.

Sid stood a few feet from him, her sleep-heavy eyes wide and soft. "Coffee," she croaked.

"I'll grab you a cup." Beck nodded to one of the stools at the counter. "Take a seat." He raised a questioning eyebrow. "Black?"

She gave him a look and sat down. "I guess you don't know everything about me after all, Mr. Jacobs."

"Let me guess. Cream and sugar."

"Bingo."

"I've got some bad news." He poured her a mug. "I've got sugar but only milk to go with it, and I'll cross fingers it doesn't curdle."

She sighed. "That is bad news, but I'm an absolute bitch and have been known to make heads roll until I get some caffeine into me. For your safety, I'll take it with milk."

He added milk. "Success. It didn't curdle."

She took the mug from him and sat back, taking small sips, as he got busy grilling their bagels to go with whatever it was he'd created in the other pan. A little salt and pepper, plus the last bit of butter he had on hand, and he was good to go.

Sid rummaged around for some plates and cutlery, and once the food was ready, they dug in. At first, they made the kind of small talk you used to fill the spaces between all that other stuff in your head—the things you either wanted to talk about or *should* be talking about.

He didn't want to bring up last night for a couple of reasons. A) It was pretty damn lame to bring a woman back to your place and then pass out on the bed while waiting for her. Shit, If the guys knew, he'd never live that one down. And B) he'd never brought anyone back to his place, and now that he was sober, it kind of confused him. He had rules for a reason.

"Hello? Where'd you go to?"

"What was that?" Beck reached for her empty plate. "Sorry, my head's still a little fuzzy."

Sidney handed him her cutlery. While he rinsed off the dishes, she poured them each another mug of coffee.

"So about last night..." She peered at him over the top of the mug.

"About last night," he repeated, leaning against the counter while she settled back onto the stool.

"I had a good time," she said softly.

"Me too."

She eyed him up, and he thought that maybe her creamy skin was a shade pinker than a few seconds earlier.

"It's probably a good thing that, um, you fell asleep so quickly."

Yep. Definitely pinker.

"Probably," he replied.

"I mean, we hardly know each other."

God, she was cute. "True." He nodded. "Though if I remember correctly, I seemed to be getting a lot right last night. So tell me something I don't know."

Her eyes widened a bit, and she ran her fingers across the rim of her mug, a slight frown on her face. "What big dark secret do I divest to a man I barely know?"

"Make sure it's a good one."

"I'll tell if you share too."

"Go for it."

"Okay." She sat back, clearly enjoying herself. "Are you ready?"

Jingle meowed loudly, and he scooped up the kitten. "So ready."

"I was born with an extra toe."

He blinked. "Big one or little one?"

"Little." She paused and flashed a grin. "You weren't expecting that one, were you?"

"Nope."

She laughed. "It usually freaks people out and I catch them trying to get a glimpse of my toes. It's not there, by the way. My parents had it removed when I was two because it hindered my balance and made it hard for me to walk." She finished her coffee and pushed the mug aside.

"Your turn. Tell me something about you I'd never guess. Not in a million years."

"Okay." He nodded and rocked back on his feet. "I was an altar boy until I was twelve."

"Not good enough." She shook her head. "Lame, actually."

"Okay. Hold on." He scratched Jingle under the chin and set her on the counter. "I've never broken a bone."

"That's surprising, I'll give you that, but still pretty lame."

"We're going hard-core, I see."

"We are."

He looked at her and grinned. "I'm not sure if you're ready for this one."

"I'm ready." She leaned forward, and Jingle jumped onto her lap.

"I can recite the entire Pledge of Allegiance."

"So can I."

"Backward."

Her right eyebrow shot up at that. "All right. That's impressive. I'm not sure why you would ever want to do that, but yes, impressive." She angled her head a bit and grinned. "What's the most embarrassing you've ever done?"

"Man, I don't think we have enough time for this." Beck grabbed her empty mug and set it in the sink. He was thinking of something he hadn't thought of in a long, long time.

"I'm man enough to admit that I'm not fond of heights. It's kind of something that comes with age. Being comfortable in admitting your faults or weaknesses. But as a teen, it was something I was embarrassed about. My senior year of high school, we had a class trip to Canada. We went to Ottawa and Toronto. When we got Toronto, we had some free time, and Cate wanted to go to the top of the CN Tower. Then some other kids wanted to come along, and how could I say no? I didn't want her to think I was a wimp. If you're not familiar with it, the structure is similar the needle in Seattle. So up I go, and there's this glass bottom on the damn thing. I took one step out and lost it. I hyperventilated, fell backward, and knocked myself out. They had to call EMS."

"Wow."

"Yeah."

"I guess it didn't matter to Cate," she said softly when he looked up. "In the end."

He shook his head and laughed. "No. She never let me forget it, but she was okay having a height-averse boyfriend." He leaned back against the counter. "What about you?"

"Oh." She made a face. "It's pretty bad."

"I'm waiting."

"I see that." She sighed. "Well, when I was a freshman in college, I hung out with a large group of friends. A mixture of guys and girls. On winter break, a bunch of us went to Colorado on a ski trip. There was this one guy, Vance was his name."

"Vance. Sounds like a serial killer."

"I know," she replied with a chuckle. "He was cute, though, with long hair and soulful eyes. He used to quote Jim Morrison poetry. Anyway, we ended up sleeping in this large open room with like, eight beds, so there were a lot of us crammed in there. He was in my bed, and you know, things were getting hot and heavy, and he, ah..."

This was gonna be good. Beck could tell. He leaned forward and waited.

"He farted. Loud and long and so gross, it made me want to vomit."

"Things happen. I mean, maybe the guy had too many greens for supper."

She looked outraged. "He could have eaten an entire cabbage patch for all I care. The guy told everyone it was me."

He hid a smile. "He didn't"

"He did. *And they believed him.* To this day, Carly, one of the girls I stayed in touch with, she calls me volcano, because apparently, it sounded like an eruption."

"I'm going to assume that was the end of your infatuation with Vance."

"Damn right it was." A wicked smile crept over her face. "Last I heard, he was in jail for tax fraud."

Beck's cell rang just then, a shrill sound that made her jump in her chair. He grabbed it from his room and read the message from Nash Booker on his way back to the kitchen.

"Everything all right?" Sid asked.

Before he could take the time to think things through, which meant before he could talk himself out of what it was he was thinking about, he glanced up at her.

"How do you feel about coming along to a sugar shack?"

"A sugar what?"

"A buddy of mine owns some property out in the bush, and his maple trees are tapped and running. With all the snow we've had the last few days, the weather is perfect for a shack party." He gave her a moment. "You in?"

"This sounds like a repeat of last night," she said softly.

"I promise I won't fall asleep on you."

She slid off the stool. "Good. I'm in."

CHAPTER TWELVE

Living all her life on the West Coast meant that Sidney had never been to a sugar shack. Heck, up until a few hours ago, she hadn't heard the term before. And now? A grin touched her mouth as she ate a snow cone doused in fresh maple syrup. Now she was a fan.

They'd spent the last four hours out on Hudson Blackwell's property, which was located high up in the hills among forests that seemed to span forever. It was a vacation property spread out over at least one hundred acres, maybe more, complete with bungalows for rent that surrounded a lake for kayaking and water sports in the summer, pond hockey and ice fishing in the winter. It wasn't Crystal Lake and not nearly as big, but for this particular slice of heaven, it was enough.

There was a good-sized gang out here, and she'd met a ton of new people. And in the gathering gloom as she stood in the shadows, warmed from the large bonfire that shot flames high into the air, she couldn't help but marvel at the buffet of men to peruse. In fact, she'd low-key taken a few pictures and sent them to her sister. Kylie had responded with a text message.

I'm on the next plane out.

Then...

Which one is your guy?

Sid stood in a group of women who'd been lovely and friendly and super inclusive: Poppy Fairbanks, Sara Blackwell, and Honey Booker. They'd made her feel welcome, which wasn't always the case when coming into a new group, and for that, she was grateful. She felt like she'd made some friends. And yet she couldn't stop staring at her guy. Her cheeks warmed at the thought. *Her guy.*

"Pretty incredible, isn't it?"

She turned and accepted a cup of hot chocolate from Poppy. "You mean the view?"

She made a comical face and laughed. "What else?"

"You do seem to have a high ratio of extremely hot men. Is it a Crystal Lake thing, or is this phenomenon statewide?"

"That I can't say. But I will tell you that I was in LA for a couple of years after college, and it's like the capital of the world for male models and wannabe actors. Trust me, every casting director I met would be drooling like crazy if they got just one peek at all that," she waved her hand dramatically, "over there."

"You were in LA?" Curious, Sid forgot about the men, in particular *her guy,* and focused on Poppy. She was a bit of a mystery. Beautiful. Super nice. Light. Always ready to help. But in the short time she'd known her, there'd been a few moments of long silences and shadowed eyes. Sid sensed something darker hidden beneath the exterior she presented and wondered about the layers she possessed.

The thing about living with pain, the kind that broke hearts and killed dreams, was that it somehow made it easier to sense in others.

Poppy averted her gaze and took a sip of cocoa. "I headed out there by myself with a Honda Civic jam-packed full of stuff, five thousand bucks in the bank, and a big dream of being an actress." She was silent for a few moments. "Turns out the city was too big for this small-town girl, so I came home."

"That takes a lot of guts. Do you miss it?"

"Sometimes. It was difficult...to give up on my dream."

Sid wondered about that. She wondered about those layers and if there was more to the story. Just then, Poppy's face paled a bit, and she bit her bottom lip.

"Shit," she muttered, taking a step back as if looking for some way to hide.

"What's wrong?" Concerned, Sidney glanced back to the group of men and spotted Link Major and a newcomer. The other man was one Sid hadn't met yet, and if she were a guy, the kind who liked to misbehave, she'd give a wolf whistle, because damn, the man carried himself in a way that screamed danger and had the looks to match.

"Who's that?" Sid asked.

"Link Major. He's, like, this soccer guy."

"I've met him. No, the other one."

"Oh." Poppy, smoothed out her long auburn hair, her actions entirely way too casual. "That's Boone Avery."

"Boone. That's an unusual name."

"His great-great, maybe another great or two, grandfather knew Daniel Boone, and there's one named in every generation of that family."

"His name sounds familiar somehow."

"He's an athlete." Poppy's gaze was locked on the man. Sidney didn't say anything else, because she was pretty sure Poppy wouldn't hear her anyway. It was obvious Boone was one of those layers she'd sensed in Poppy, and it was none of her business.

Nash Booker, Hudson Blackwell, and Beck wandered over a few minutes later, and all those butterflies that had been playing havoc with her stomach intensified to the point she couldn't finish her hot chocolate.

"You having a good time?" Beck asked quietly.

"I am. Your friends are great. All of them. Really." She paused and made sure Poppy was out of earshot. "What's the story with Boone Avery? And why do I feel like I know him?"

Beck's eyebrows shot up in surprise, but he quickly recovered. "He played pro ball out of college. Was a first-round draft pick for New Orleans and came damn close to leading the team to the Super Bowl a couple years back. He is, or rather he was, one of the top quarterbacks in the league, but he up and quit when his dad got sick last year, and after he died, he stuck around. His wife stayed for a couple of months but then she left him and headed back to New Orleans, leaving their kid here with Boone."

"So he's raising a child on his own?"

"Yeah. A little boy from what I heard."

"It's amazing, isn't it?" she murmured.

"What's that?" Beck moved closer so that his body blocked everyone, and with the flames shooting fire behind him, his features were in shadow.

She looked up at him and in the darkness found his eyes. "It doesn't matter who we are. Or where we're from. Or what we've accomplished in life. Nothing's a guarantee. Certainly not happiness."

"You're right," he said, moving even closer. "Any one of us can lose the thing we value the most. That thing we need just to breathe. Sometimes without even knowing."

She licked her suddenly dry lips. The air shifted, or thickened or something, because all of a sudden, she found it hard to breathe.

"We should go," she whispered. She couldn't take her eyes off him. She was flooded with desire and the need to connect with this man. Sid didn't want to analyze or think or discuss. She wanted to act. She wanted to be alone with Beck. To see where this would go.

Beck didn't say a word. He grabbed her hand, and they said their goodbyes and suited up for the Ski-Doo. Sidney was very aware that a lot of the folks behind were watching as she slid onto the Ski-Doo behind him. They were wondering and thinking and discussing. And damn, but she wanted to give them something to think about.

She waved goodbye to Poppy and held on as Beck navigated the powerful machine out of the clearing and onto the main trail that followed the lake down and then cut through the forest all the way to Crystal Lake. It was cold, that small window between dusk and nightfall, and she shivered and hunkered as close to Beck as she could.

But deep inside, there where her heart beat fast and hard, she was on fire. Her blood sang with molten lava, her skin flushed with heat, and between her legs, a pulse began to ache, an insistent throb that didn't let up. By the time they got to the stone cottage, she was a mess. The feel of his broad shoulders and hard body pressed up against hers was almost too much. She needed to make a move now, or let this moment slip away forever.

The Ski-Doo slid to a stop, and for a second or two, all she heard was her heart thumping inside her head. Then Beck cut the engine and looked at her over his shoulder. He slid his helmet back and waited.

"Are you..." God, she couldn't get the words out. "Do you want..." Her mouth was too dry, her nerves too shot.

"I brought you back here because I didn't want to assume some things." He watched her intently.

She licked her lips. "What would those things be?" Thank the Lord and all that's holy, she could get a damn sentence out.

"The kind of things a guy is not supposed to assume." He flashed a wicked grin. "The kind of things that guy has been thinking about since last night."

"Would those things involve a guy and a girl?"

"Yeah. They would."

"Would those things be physical?"

He nodded.

Her breath caught. She was enjoying this flirtation more than chocolate-and-peanut-butter ice cream, and everyone knew that chocolate and peanut butter together was bliss.

"Would they include getting naked?"

His nostrils flared. "Definitely."

That ache between her legs intensified at the timbre of his voice, and it took everything she had not to groan or moan or make a complete idiot out of herself.

"So, let me get this straight. you brought me back here because you didn't want to take me to your place, on account of the fact you didn't want to assume I'd be up for some of those physical, naked things you want to do?"

"With you," he added with a wink. "The things I have in mind are kind of hard to do on my own."

"I see," she replied.

"It's a dilemma."

"There's only one way to fix it."

"I'm open to suggestions." Gone was the teasing tone to Beck's voice. He looked at her in a way that was primal. Like he wanted to eat her. And just like that, the pulse and throb became too much, and she wiggled a bit until she got some relief.

"Take me back to your place." She wrapped her arms around him again and snuggled in close. "We can start with the naked thing."

CHAPTER THIRTEEN

The ride back from Hudson's house was the longest ride he'd taken in months. Years, maybe. He and Sid had been dancing around this thing between them since the night before, and the thought of getting her into his bed was making the trip back painful.

He was hard as fuck and as horny as a teenager, and his erection didn't lessen on the way home. Not with Sid pressed up against his back and her arms wrapped around his midsection like she was holding on for dear life. Which she very could well could have been, because he was traveling a lot faster than he should be.

But the erection and the electric thoughts inside his head reduced him to the Neanderthal he supposed all men were. At the most basic level, men wanted one thing most of the time. And he was taking a beautiful woman back to his place, and there would be nakedness involved, and sex. And hopefully lots of it.

Damn, he couldn't remember the last time he'd been this worked up over a woman. *Other than Cate.*

The thought came to him real sneaky like, and he immediately pushed it away. Cate was different from everyone else, and no way was he going there tonight. This was just sex.

He pulled his sled right up to the front door and cut the engine. Kind of a lame move, but hell, it was a bit of a hike from the shop, and the situation between his legs didn't make that possible. He was going to have a hard enough time getting into the house without alerting Sid to the fact that he had the mother of all erections going on inside his pants.

He waited for her to get off the Ski-Doo and then followed suit, giving her the lead to walk up to the door. Once inside, he was immediately attacked by Jingle, who meowed as if he'd left her for weeks instead of just the afternoon.

"Hey there," he said, stepping out of his boots and yanking off his jacket. He set them aside, along with his helmet, and told Sid he needed to look after the kitten. He took Jingle to the mudroom and spent a good minute or two talking down his erection before he was able to feed the cat and top up her water.

"You need to be good tonight," he said softly. "And I'm closing the bedroom door."

He left the little girl eating and purring happily and made his way back to the living room. But no Sid.

Confused, he turned in a circle before he had an *ah-ha* moment.

With a grin, he strode down the hallway, his breath hitching a bit when he saw the light on in his bedroom. He'd taken exactly one step inside when his world tipped a bit, and the situation between his legs went from standby to code fucking red. He froze, and his eyes roved over every inch of her body. Her naked, hot-as-hell body.

Hair that was silky and shone in the low light.

Breasts that were round and high. Not too big and not too small, but just the way he liked them.

Rounded hips.

Long legs.

And a little bit of hair down there. Just enough to entice and make his mouth water.

"We said we'd start with the naked thing." She licked her bottom lip and looked at him with hooded eyes.

"We did." He sounded like a beast and practically growled.

"So get naked."

"You're sassy," he said, yanking his sweater off and tossing it aside. "I like sassy."

"I've been called worse."

"I bet." His jeans were next.

"You seem a little worked up." Her words were throaty and did something to him. He swore his cock twitched, and when he glanced up, she was focused on said cock with an intensity that made his blood sing. He stepped out of his boxers and walked toward Sidney, his body tense and hot and so full of need, it was painful.

He didn't answer her. In fact, he didn't say another word. He sank his hands into all that hair around her face and claimed her mouth in a kiss that made his head spin. She tasted like chocolate and mint and candy. And she was so damn warm and soft, he could spend the next hour kissing her. But he didn't have an hour, and there was something else he wanted to taste before he looked after himself.

He tore his mouth from hers and then dipped to her breasts. He licked around the nipple of each of them before sucking hard, and then moving her back toward his bed. She didn't resist; in fact, she felt like liquid silk in his hands as she fell back on the bed, eyes half-open, mouth swollen from his kisses.

He pulled her close to the edge and spread her knees wide. "Let me see," he said roughly. He fell to his knees and moved between her legs. "You're beautiful." Beck put his mouth on her. He tasted and tugged and suckled and worshiped her with his mouth and hands until her body began to shudder and he knew she was close. Her fingers were in his hair, and when she came, she held him there like the queen she was, and Beck was good enough to let her think she was controlling the situation. But after a few moments, his need was too great. His cock too hard. His brain too loud with a voice telling him to take her now.

"God, Beck," she whispered, watching him.

"You like that."

She nodded.

"Babe, we're just starting."

He got to his feet and grabbed a condom from the drawer by his bed, then glanced over to her. Her inner thighs glistened with her desire, and the smell of sex was already thick in the air. His gut pulled, and his shoulders clenched.

He walked over to the bed and kissed her once more, encouraging her to move and give him some room, before positioning himself between her legs. "This is going to be fast and hard." He teased her, his hands on her breasts, rubbing her nipples while he pushed at her opening. "But I promise the next time will last longer."

Beck slid inside her with one thrust, and damn, but she felt good. She was slick and tight, and she closed around him until he groaned. Sweat beaded his brow as he began to move inside her, slowly at first, because he knew this would be his only first time with Sid, and there was something about a first time with a woman a guy needed to to pay attention to.

This one was worth savoring.

But Beck was only human, and he picked up the rhythm, their bodies both slick with sweat and in sync. She met his thrusts head-on, and he rocked into her over and over, all that heat and friction almost too much to bear.

"I'm going to come," he said, dipping his head for a taste of her breast. "I can't hold back."

She answered by digging her nails into his butt and urging him on with a passion to match his own. They raced to the end, and when they both came, Beck, literally saw stars. He emptied himself and looked up at the ceiling, blinking away the red haze that had overtaken him. Then he collapsed and pulled her with him, burying his head in the side of her neck.

"That was..." He struggled for air.

"I know," she murmured.

Jingle began to meow and jump up at the side of the bed, and he cursed, looking over his shoulder. "Forgot to close the door." He rolled off the bed and padded through to the bathroom, where he took care of the condom and then locked his little buddy in the mudroom. He felt bad, but not bad enough that he wanted the kitten watching him and Sid have sex, or to listen to her meowing her fool head off wanting up on the bed.

He went to the kitchen and grabbed two beers from the fridge and the last bag of plain chips from his cupboard.

When he returned to his bedroom, Sid was sitting with the blankets pulled over her breasts. He held up the chips and beer. "It's not much, but it's all I got."

He slid in beside her and handed her one of the cans.

"Well, this is a first," she said with a giggle. "Beer and chips in bed."

"I'm not fancy, that's for sure."

"Fancy is overrated." She glanced his way. "Tell me something about yourself."

He chuckled. "We're playing this game again, are we?"

"It's a good way to get to know each other." She paused. "Your name, for instance."

"What about it?"

She swallowed a chip and took a sip of beer. "It's unusual. I don't think I've ever heard the name before."

"Here's the thing," he replied. "Beck is an old name in the

family on my mother's side. He was her great-uncle and more like a father to her. So you could say my name was preordained. I could have been born a girl and I think she still would have named me Beckworth."

"Beckworth?" Her right eyebrow rose.

"Mouthful, right?"

She laughed, and he liked the sound of it. Maybe a little too much, but right now, he wasn't going to dwell on that. She dipped the can back and finished it on one long draw.

"Impressive," Beck said, finishing his own.

"Well, I'm recharged and ready."

"For what, exactly?" But she was already tossing aside the covers, and he reached for her.

"For the next time, remember?" Sid nipped at his neck and bent close to his ear. "You said it would last longer, and I'm going to hold you to that."

"That sounds like a challenge."

"Call it whatever you want."

It was definitely a challenge, and Beck was up for it. He went slower and longer, and then he did it all over again. And when he finally fell away from her, exhausted, he drifted off to sleep, and in the night, his arms reached for Sidney. He didn't know it yet, but he'd remember this moment later. The feel of it. The rightness to it.

He'd remember and wonder why he let it slip away.

CHAPTER FOURTEEN

Sidney's eyes slowly opened. At first, she didn't know where she was because the room was dark, though she noticed a sliver of light that fell from underneath the shades covering the window. Then she noticed something heavy across her leg, and that something heavy was attached to a male body snuggled up behind her. At just about the time she noticed the leg, she remembered *exactly* where she was.

Holy hell. She slammed her eyes shut and replayed the high points of last night.

Beck Jacobs's mouth on her. *Downtown.*

His hands all over. Every. Single. Inch.

His body inside hers.

His dark eyes.

His slow smile.

The muscles in his shoulders.

The shape of his butt.

Carefully, she turned over so that she faced him, and now that her eyes had adjusted to the gloom, she was able to make out his features.

Beck was deep asleep, his breaths long and even, his handsome features relaxed. She saw a glimmer of the younger man he must have been, and then noticed a small scar not far from his right temple. Her fingers found themselves drawn to it, and she traced the faint line gently. He had great bone structure, could have been a model, and his mouth was to die for. She leaned up and swept her lips across his.

He was, quite simply, breathtaking.

Sidney watched him sleep for a long time, long enough for her body to liquefy and for that need he'd sated the night before to come alive again. She grinned and pushed at him until he was on his back. She took her time because she didn't want to wake him just yet. Beck mumbled something unintelligible but didn't open his eyes.

"You will, my friend," she whispered, pushing the blankets back. The air was chilled, and goose bumps erupted across her skin as she kissed his torso and moved lower, and then lower still. Until she took him in her mouth and began to knead and suckle. It didn't take long for Beck to harden, and once he was ready, she straddled him and sank onto his cock, groaning at the feel of him inside her.

He filled so completely. She sat there for a few seconds and tried to calm her breathing, because this feeling was one she wanted to remember. She enjoyed the sensation of him inside her, loved how it felt. His hands had crept up to her hip; he was stirring, but his eyes were still closed. His chest rose and fell, a bit quicker than before, but he was still caught somewhere between sleep and awake, probably dreaming about sex.

She began to move, her body awash with desire as she found the perfect rhythm, her senses inflamed at the guttural sound that came from deep inside Beck. He sounded like an animal.

"God damn." His eyes flew open, and she saw the confusion at first, then the desire and the need he made no attempt to hide.

"Good morning," she managed to say as she rose and fell

above him. "Since we were already naked, I thought we could do the sex thing again." She arched her back and bit her lip when his thumb found her clit and began to massage her. "You don't mind?" Her words ended on a groan as the first ripple of an orgasm teased her.

"Not at all." His voice was rough, his words clipped.

After that, there was no more talking. There were groans and moans and some swearing. When her orgasm built, when layers of pleasure wrapped themselves around her, his hands gripped her so hard, she was sure there'd be bruising. Did she care? Hell no.

This was, without a doubt, the best sex of her life.

Sid had him one more time in the shower, and an hour later, they walked into the kitchen, Jingle scampering along behind them, her little meows sharp.

"Coffee?" Beck asked.

She was starving, but she knew he didn't have any food. "Sure." She made a face. Or cream.

Jingle meowed until she picked her up and cuddled the kitten in silence, suddenly feeling vulnerable. In the bedroom, they'd been enveloped by a cocoon of shadows, but out here, the sun shone, and there was no hiding.

Beck handed her a mug and stood on the other side of the island, bent over with his elbows resting on top of it.

"Last night was incredible." He said the words so quietly, so sincerely, that she was taken by surprise. Since when had she been with a man who owned such candor? Who wasn't afraid to expose himself this way? The first time she'd been with Nick, he didn't call her for a full week because (she found out afterward) he didn't want her to know how much he was into her. This right here? This was refreshing.

"It kinda was," she replied shyly, looking at everything except Beck.

"So," he said, taking a sip of coffee. "What's your story, Sidney Barrett?"

"My story?" She kept her voice light, even though this, the exchanging of history, was anything but light. Not after a night of the kind of sex and connection they'd shared.

"Why did you come to Crystal Lake?"

God, where to start?

"I came here to recharge my batteries. I've had a pretty intense couple of years, and things happened, some bad things, and I needed a break. I just...I wasn't present, you know?" She glanced up. "My mind wasn't working the way I needed it to for my business, and I was talking to Nate about a project and somehow spilled everything to him. He told me that Crystal Lake was the remedy I needed." She shrugged. "The thought of being someplace where no one knew me, a place where I could kind of hide, was attractive, and then when Nathan sent me a picture of the stone cottage, I fell in love with it."

"And your family?"

Jingle began to squirm. Beck reached for her and automatically cradled the kitten against his chest. Honestly. It should be illegal for someone as big and handsome and male as

Beck Jacobs to stand in front of her, looking all, well, *big and handsome and male*, while holding on to a tiny kitten.

She took a moment and tried to compose her thoughts.

"Sid?" His gentle tone tugged on all kinds of things inside her.

"I'm not used to this," she admitted.

"Used to what?"

"This sharing thing." With a man she'd just had sex with. A man she'd only known for a week.

"If you're uncomfortable, you don't have to say anything." He was giving her an out, which said a lot. As well as being honest and open, the guy was caring.

She toyed with her mug for a few seconds and then dove in. "I have a sister, Kylie. She's crazy, though I love her to pieces in spite of how crazy she is. She's like this big romantic, always looking for the grand gesture, and she's been in love more times than anyone I know. She has a heart of gold and would do anything for me. She's my best friend."

Sid took a sip of the bitter brew but didn't taste it, too caught up in thoughts and memories. "My dad died when I was sixteen, and my mom is remarried to a great guy. His name is Frank. He has this big scruffy beard and a handlebar mustache."

"A legit handlebar?"

"You heard me correctly. A handlebar. It took some getting used to, and he's nothing like my father, he's more of a rough guy where my dad was polished. He was a partner in one of the biggest law firms on the West Coast. My dad was awesome, but he got sick and died, and Mom met Frank on holiday, a *P.S. I Love You,* kind of holiday. She was in Ireland by herself, driving along some winding road out in the middle of nowhere, and her car broke down. Frank wandered by, and she stayed in Ireland on an extended vacation. They got married the following year." Her voice trailed off, and then she shrugged. "I don't see her very often, but we FaceTime a lot."

"Sounds like a good excuse to go to Ireland."

She nodded. "It's beautiful where they are."

Beck topped up their coffee mugs. "What's a *P.S. I Love You* holiday? I haven't heard of that particular one."

"It's based on a movie, which was based on a book, and maybe someday, we can watch it together."

Jesus. Mary. And Joseph.

Did she just say that? Did she just suggest a movie night? As if whatever this was they were doing was going to continue? As if a guy like Beck would sit and watch a chick flick with her? She hung her head, a little embarrassed, which was saying something considering they'd had sex more times in twenty-four hours than she'd ever had before with anyone. Nick included.

"I'm not much of a movie guy," he replied.

Shit. This was it. The big brush-off.

"But I'd find it hard to say no to spending another night with you."

Sid's head shot up, and the look in his eye was enough to set her panties on fire. She squirmed a little, which was the wrong thing to do because it only made the friction between her legs that much worse.

How could she still want him so badly when it had been less than an hour since the last time he'd been inside her?

"So what are we doing here, Beck?" She held her breath, knowing that every single word that came from his mouth would be honest.

"We're getting to know each other."

"Okay."

He rested his palms on the counter and leaned closer. "And the getting-to-know-each-other thing involves physical activities."

"Physical is good."

"And then there's the other part."

"What's that, exactly?"

His smiled, that devastating wicked grin that made her heart melt. "That's the part we're figuring out. We've got the physical thing down pat."

"And then some," she murmured.

His grin widened. "We should maybe practice some of the other stuff."

"Like what?" God, she loved talking to this man.

"How about dinner?" He grimaced and looked behind her. "I'm low on supplies right now, but I can grab something when I'm in town before I head back here."

"Why don't you come to the cottage?"

"I don't like to leave Jingle alone."

"That's fine, just bring her."

He watched her for a few moments. "Yeah?"

Sidney nodded and slipped from her stool. "Yes. She'll be good company for me."

"Okay." Beck leaned closer and dropped a devastating kiss on her mouth. "Let me grab my coat and some tools I need for the day, and I'll take you home."

Sid stretched and smiled at the aches and pains she felt. They were the good kind. The Beck kind. She wandered over to the living room and spied a photo on the table there. A quick glance behind told her she was still alone, so she crept closer. It was Beck, a much younger version, with his arm around a woman's shoulder, smiling down at her. He was shirtless—the photo looked like it had been taken down at the lake—and her head was averted so Sidney couldn't see her face.

But it was the expression on his that made the photo. It was such obvious, unrestrained love that it made her ache inside. It was the kind of look every woman on the planet wanted. The kind that said, *I love you*. The kind that said, *I give every corner of my heart to you*.

For someone so young to have that? For a girl to inspire that kind of devotion and depth in a young man? It said a lot. Beck had loved his Cate something fierce, even as young as they were. It made Sid wonder.

What did it feel like to have someone look at you like that? To know you held their heart in your hands? To have that kind of power was scary, and to give it up was scarier.

Would she ever experience a love like that?

"You ready?" Beck's voice echoed from down the hall.

She jumped and then got busy with her boots, which were at the front door. "Yes."

He came up beside her and reached for the door. "Let's go."

She slid into his truck, and though they made small talk on the way over to the cottage, the only thing in her mind was that photo and maybe the feeling that she'd just stepped into something.

And that something was going to bite her in the ass if she wasn't careful.

CHAPTER FIFTEEN

Over the next few weeks, Beck and Sidney fell into a pattern. His days were spent working on a new kitchen for a client, while his evenings were spent at the stone cottage with Sidney. Hell, even the kitten spent most of her time there. This thing between them was more than a flirtation. More than two people physically attracted to each other.

It was moving in a direction he wasn't entirely sure he was comfortable with, but he couldn't seem to stop himself. In the space of a month, Sidney Barrett had become the kind of drug he didn't seem capable of giving up.

Simply put, he didn't want to.

Case in point...

A few days earlier, a couple of his buddies called him up because there was a spot open for one lucky bastard to fly with them up to northern Canada for a week of ice fishing. Apparently, Armstrong had backed out because his wife threatened to kick him out for good if he left her alone while he was off fishing with the guys. Now, Beck was the kind of man who liked to fish. It didn't matter if it was an early morning in the summer or a late afternoon in the fall or way the hell up north in a small ice hut with a bunch of guys on a lake in the middle of nowhere. But he made up some dumb-ass work-related excuse and thanked them for the offer, but politely declined.

Beck thought about that as he carried his tools from Mrs. Havernash's house and placed them in the back of his truck. He guessed that right about now, the boys were on to beer, food, gossip, and as many off-color jokes as they could come up with after a full day fishing. And here he was finishing up a job and getting ready to meet Sidney at the Coach House for beer and wings and then a jaunt down to the river and boardwalk.

"You get everything finished, Beckworth?"

He turned and gave a quick nod as he headed back to the house for the last of it. Mrs. Havernash had been his Sunday school teacher and the secretary at the elementary school he'd attended, and she always used his Christian name.

"Got the backsplash finished, and that was the last thing on our list." He stepped up on the porch and paused. The woman had just celebrated her eightieth birthday and was as spry and quick as she'd always been. Her hair was snow white, the wiry curls cut real short, and her tiny frame was wrapped up in a blue dress with yellow flowers and big old cardigan that looked about two sizes too big for her. Beck had never seen the woman in a pair of pants.

"Don't go touching it, now," he said with a quick smile. "The grout has to cure, and I'll be back in a couple of days to give it a wash and seal the edges."

"It looks wonderful. Oh, I was excited when my son, Danny, told me he was paying to have my kitchen redone. I swear I haven't spent a dime on it since Mr. Havernash passed, and that was nearly twenty-five years ago."

"The place looks spiffy, Mrs. H, and I think you did a real good job with the materials you decided on."

"Bah," she said, shaking her head. "You made all the

suggestions. All I did was nod and say, 'Whatever you think is best.'" She cocked her head a bit and handed him the canvas bag he'd come back for. "How's your brother doing with those babies on the way?"

"You know how Nate is. He's never good at waiting on things, and nine months is a long time."

Mrs. Havernash chuckled. "Don't I know it. Why, I remember once when he was about six or maybe seven, and we had the Christmas pageant at church. He was one of the wise men, and in the last segment. I swear he had ants in his pants the entire time we had to wait backstage. When it was finally time for the wise men to walk onto the stage, he pushed his way through, so anxious to get out there first, and knocked over Jesus, Mary, and Joseph. Can you believe that?"

"I can. If I remember right, after he took out the manger, he fell off the stage."

Her face crinkled up, and she slowly nodded. "I think you're right."

Beck took a step back. He liked Mrs. Havernash a lot, and he knew the lady was lonely, that her Danny had only paid for the renovation because the guy felt guilty he never saw his mother. Normally, Beck would take the time to chat with her, but he glanced at his watch. He was already twenty minutes late, and Sid was already at the Coach House.

"Look at me keeping you here when a young man like yourself must have plans this evening." She gave him a knowing look. "I've heard you've been keeping company with the woman who's been staying out at the stone cottage."

The gossip mill in Crystal Lake never failed to amaze him.

"I'm meeting Sidney for dinner." There was no point in denial. Heck, the rumor mill probably had them shacked up and on the way to the altar.

Her eyes softened. "It's about time, Beckworth. You're too

good of a man to still be on your own. Now you go on and make sure to give my best to your brother and Molly."

He took another step back.

"Oh, and tell your mother that I should be able to volunteer next week at the hospital. Now that this nasty chest cold is gone, I do love being a baby cuddler."

"I will."

He tossed the canvas bag in the back of his truck, closed the cover, and gave one more wave before he hopped inside. He hauled ass to the Coach House. It had been a long day trying to finish up this job before the weekend. He was thirsty and hungry, and, no way around it, he was looking forward to spending the evening with Sid.

The parking lot was packed when he pulled up, but Beck managed to find a spot at the back. He glanced down at his work jeans and boots—he'd had no time to run home and change—and they'd have to do.

The smell of beer and grease hit him full-on when he walked inside and spied Nash, the owner, almost immediately. He was behind the bar chatting with a bear of a man who went by the name of Tiny. Nash looked up, lifted his chin, and pointed to his left, and Beck strode through the crowd, eyes already on the woman who was waiting on him.

Her hair was loose and hung around her shoulders, the way he liked it, and she wore a simple formfitting black top, tucked into faded jeans, and black boots. A long sliver chain was the only jewelry she wore, and her lips, oh man, her lips were painted a deep, sexy red.

She glanced up just then, and he smiled, almost to her, when a hand reached out and grabbed him.

He turned to his right, and his smile slowly faded when he laid eyes on Emily Davenport. She sat alone at the table.

"Hey," he said, casually, aware that Sid's eyes were on him.

This felt awkward as hell. It wasn't exactly a situation Beck found himself in a lot.

"Hey yourself," she replied. She looked past him and then swung her gaze back. "So the rumors are true."

"Look, Em." God, he felt like a shit. "I...we..."

"No, don't say anything, Beck." Her soft, sad eyes were full of something he didn't recognize or understand. "She seems lovely, and I'm glad for you."

"It's not..." The denial was hot on his tongue, but the words died, and he stood there feeling like an idiot.

"It's not what? Serious? It doesn't have to be. You've taken a step, and that's the important thing. I hope." She sighed and shook her head. "I hope you find what you've been looking for all these years. You deserve it."

Her mother appeared just then, and after he said a quick hello, Beck headed for Sidney. He sat down across from her and grabbed the beer she'd been good enough to order. He took a long drink, his mind a little addled, his thoughts a little chaotic.

"Who was that?" Sid asked softly. "I remember seeing her the night of the hockey game. She stopped you then too."

"Her name is Emily."

Sid took a sip of beer and looked Emily's way again. "She's very attractive."

"She is."

"You guys were involved?"

Beck set down his beer. Another guy could lie and sweep things under the rug in order to avoid a possible sticky situation.

"We were. For a time. But it's over now."

"Since..."

He looked her straight in the eye. "Since you."

She looked surprised and then licked her lips, unable to hide the small smile that touched them.

"You're nothing like any of the men I've known. You're so..."

She shook her head and grabbed a chip from the bowl. "You don't water anything down. You tell the truth."

"Lying takes too much energy. I think if you live your life hiding behind lies, you'd be damn exhausted. And life is already exhausting." He leaned close. "So why don't we order some food."

"Already done."

"Wings and fries?"

"And onion rings."

"That's my girl." He winked. "We can eat and get out of here and get back to the cottage."

"For dessert?" Her eyebrows shot up.

He nodded. "For dessert."

"Okay." Sidney grinned. "But remember, I wanted to go down to the river. Molly said the local youth group is selling hot chocolate to raise money for a trip."

"We can do that."

"Good." She licked her lips. "And Beck?"

"Yeah?"

"Leave room for lots of dessert."

"I will if you will."

Her answer was the kind of look that set his blood on fire. The waitress appeared with their order, but Beck was already thinking of dessert.

CHAPTER SIXTEEN

Sid was happy.

She was that girl.

The one who walked on clouds and sang in the shower. The woman who daydreamed and looked up recipes on the internet and attempted to cook meals thought up by Michelin-star chefs in France. She doodled in the margins of her work pad, cranked easy-listening '70s when she was alone, sported at least three new wrinkles from smiling, *and she didn't care.*

Not one bit.

In her world, the birds sang sweetly, the lake shimmered like diamonds, baby deer ran through her backyard, and Beck was in her bed every single night.

As she walked down the path that followed the river, her arm tucked into Beck's, she thought that she was the happiest girl in the world. Was it the Michigan air? The first buds on the trees and the flock of blue jays and cardinals in her backyard? The warm sun that lit the stone cottage every morning?

She glanced up at Beck. Or was it the man beside her?

It wasn't a question, really. It was all those things. But more than anything, it was the past letting go of her. Those dark times were locked up in a box she could open if need be, but locked up all the same. She wasn't ignoring them anymore. She wasn't wallowing in self-pity and pain and going through the motions of life. She wasn't thinking of what could have been before and of what she'd lost. For the first time in a long time, she was thinking about the future.

A scary thought, but also an exciting one. She was alive and grateful for what she'd allowed herself to experience. Because it wasn't so long ago that she would have been afraid to dive into this thing with Beck.

They walked along the path in silence, the chilled air refreshing as they made their way over to the Caboose, which was parked along the river. There was a lineup for hot chocolate, and Beck stopped just short of the crowd.

"It's going to be a bit of a wait," he said, turning to her. "Are you sure you want to do this?"

It *was* late. She grinned slyly. They could go back to the cottage and have all that dessert they'd been talking about at dinner. Heck, she was good for at least two servings. She giggled. Maybe three.

Sid glanced back to the Caboose and was about to tell Beck they could leave when she caught an older woman watching them intently. The woman was there with a man, most likely her husband, Sid thought, though he was busy chatting up another couple. The woman, however, was focused on Sid and Beck. She said something to the man, and he glanced over as she moved away from them and headed in their direction.

She felt Beck tense, but didn't have a chance to say anything before the woman was there, smiling at them, a sad sort of smile that didn't quite reach her eyes.

Sid let her arm fall from Beck's, and he enveloped the woman in a hug, the kind that was strong and hard and full of things unsaid.

"Hey, Colleen. I see you and Ben are here for the hot chocolate too."

The woman, Colleen, stood back and nodded. "We are." She turned to Sid and offered her hand. "I don't think we've met. I'm Colleen McBride."

McBride.

Sid took the woman's hand. "I'm Sid."

McBride. Beck had just hugged the woman like she was family. This had to be Cate's mother.

"I think I might have met your son, Ike, a few weeks back. At the hockey thing...weekend...tournament?"

Colleen nodded. "Ike and the boys sure do like their hockey." She glanced back at Beck. "Though he'd hate for me to tell you that he could barely walk for days after playing so much in one weekend."

"I hear that," Beck replied. "We're not getting younger."

"No," Colleen murmured. "We're not." She stepped back. "I should go. I just wanted to say hello. It's been a while. You know our door is always open, Beck. Same as it's always been."

"Yeah. I'm... Work's been crazy lately." Beck ran his hands through his hair. "I'll get over soon. I promise."

She looked at Sid. "Nice meeting you."

She headed back to the group of folks she'd been waiting with, and the man waved to Beck before he and his wife moved up the line for their hot chocolate.

"We can go home," Sid whispered. Beck's face was unreadable, his mouth set, his eyes hooded.

"Let's go," he said, turning around to head back to the parking lot. He didn't reach for her or touch her, and that happiness she'd felt only a few minutes earlier dimmed. She might be able to say goodbye to her past and all the ghosts that lingered there, but it was clear that Beck couldn't.

The ride back to the lake was quiet. By the time they

reached her cottage, Sid's shoulders were tense, her stomach upset, and she was almost certain that, for the first time in weeks, she'd be sleeping alone.

She'd practiced a little speech on the ride back. It was full of things like, *take some time, Beck, it's okay*, and, *I'll understand if you need to be alone*, or, *I'm here for you, however you need.*

But he surprised her. He pulled up, cut the engine, and was out of his truck before she had a chance to say any of those things. But the unsaid words and thoughts were there between them. She felt them hovering like a spectre. And for the first time since she'd started whatever it was with Beck, she felt off balance. Like the rug was about to be pulled out from under her.

She followed him inside the cottage and started to unbutton her jacket, trying to form the words she needed to say. She knew she had to deal with all the unsaid things, because not dealing with them meant they'd fester. And festering wounds could spread until nothing could fix them.

But Beck had other plans. He grabbed something from his jacket and strode toward the television and media center. She followed him and sank onto the sofa, stroking Jingle, who'd come from nowhere and was now big enough to jump onto furniture.

Beck flicked on the gas fireplace, grabbed a remote, and came to her, sliding up beside her so she could lean into him. He aimed the remote and pressed a few buttons.

"I picked this up earlier today," he murmured.

The sound of his voice loosened all that anxiety inside her. It was warm and intimate, and she felt silly for thinking there was anything wrong. The aloofness she thought he'd displayed earlier was all in her head. Nothing more.

When the opening scenes of *P.S. I Love You* started to play, she melted into him, touched that he remembered.

"You do know this is a chick flick?" she asked softly, glancing up to find his dark eyes on her.

"I figured as much."

Her smiled slowly faltered as the plot ran through her mind. She thought of Holly and her pain when Gerry died. *Crap.* The movie would hit just a little too close to home for Beck. She wiggled a bit and sat straighter.

"We don't have to watch it. Honestly, we can go straight to dessert."

"I can handle a chick flick, and trust me, we'll get to dessert." He dropped a kiss to her nose. "Eventually."

"This one is sad before it gets a happy ending. Like, really sad." She didn't want to watch this with him.

He slowly nodded. "I know. I read the back of the DVD." He pulled her close again, and because she didn't want to cause a scene, Sidney didn't say another word. They watched the movie, and she tried not to cry, but of course, she did. When the final scene passed and it was done, Beck laid her out on the sofa and kissed her until her head spun. He nuzzled her neck and worshipped her with his mouth and hands and their clothes ended up on the floor and it was skin on skin.

They made love right there in the family room, and afterward, lying in blankets on the thick carpet in front of the fireplace, she felt some of those unsaid things bubbling up inside her.

"I didn't tell you the whole story," Sid said, gazing up at him.

"About what?" He was on his side, leaning on his elbow. Since she had his complete attention, it felt like the right time.

"My story. I only told you half of it."

"Okay." He watched her intently. She dropped her eyes, looking inside for the courage she needed to share something so painful with him.

"Two years ago, I was involved with a man, Nick. He was this larger-than-life guy with big dreams and a big personality to match. He'd played pro ball for the Giants and worked for their organization, and we had this exciting life that's hard to describe. My business had hit a plateau that I didn't think was possible. I'd just signed a distribution deal for television. This man who seemed perfect, a man who said he loved me, was at my side for this wild ride. We got engaged and then I got pregnant, and..."

Her chin trembled as she thought back. She had to take a moment to find the calm she needed in order to finish the story.

"And everything fell apart. Turns out Nick wasn't the guy I thought he was. He'd been cheating on me with a cheerleader for the Forty-Niners. I had no idea, and to make things worse, he had a kid with this other woman, and apparently didn't want another one with me. He demanded I get rid of it, but by then, I was already in love with this life growing inside me. I ended things with Nick and prepared to have a baby on my own.

"I was lucky enough to be able to afford it, so I hired this expensive designer, Pierre from Montreal, to fly out to San Diego and design the cutest nursery. I worked with him on designs. Kylie came with me to Lamaze, and Mom planned on coming home for the birth with Frank. Things were good. I was good. And then, at seven months, I went to my OB for a checkup, and there was no heartbeat."

Beck reached for her, swiping at a single tear that fell from her eye. She leaned into his palm.

"I didn't tell anyone. I couldn't. They scheduled my delivery a few days later. I got up that morning, and I remember it felt like I was in a dream. I felt like Nick should know, so I called him and I told him our baby had gone, and he was so kind. He told me he'd come with me so I wouldn't have to be alone. Said he'd meet me at the hospital."

Her voice caught. "Of course he didn't show. I labored for twenty-one hours, and I had my baby boy. He was perfect. He looked like he was sleeping. I held him for as long as they'd let me, and then I went home to a house with a nursery that would remain empty. And after that, I kind of fell away from life."

"Oh, Sid. I'm so sorry."

"You're no stranger to heartache either."

"No," he admitted softly. "I'm not."

She exhaled, and though the memories were sad, she felt lighter. "I thought my life was over. I really did. I couldn't find the joy no matter where I looked. The joy was just gone. And then I came here, and..."

She reached for him and cupped his face between her hands. "And then I came here and met you, and I realized that I'm not dead inside. Not anymore. So thank you for that."

She kissed him again as desire and want and need and love flooded her body with heat. Beck slowly slid over her, and then he was inside her, and as he rocked into her, his eyes never left hers. He kissed her, the sweetest, lightest kiss imaginable. As she raced toward an orgasm, she thought that she'd never felt so complete.

That maybe she'd cancel her flight back to San Diego on Monday. A flight that had been booked since before she'd come here. A flight she'd forgotten about until the alert on her phone at dinner.

She thought that maybe she should stick around and see where things led. That maybe she was in love.

And that this time, it was the real deal.

CHAPTER SEVENTEEN

Most Sundays, the Jacobs family gathered for dinner at either Beck's parents' place or out at Nate's. For the last month or so, Beck had missed every single one of them, and he knew that sooner or later, he'd catch crap from his mother.

He was hoping it would be later. And not in person.

But of course, that wasn't how things worked out.

His Sunday had started out pretty damn good too. He'd woken up with Sidney, and they'd had sex in the shower. Hot. Wet. Sex. And then they'd gone out for breakfast at The Breakfast Corner, a great all-day breakfast place the next county over. He'd chosen it because it cut down on the chance of bumping into folks he knew. And after last night, he wasn't ready to deal with any of that. Running into Colleen had shaken him a bit, and for the life of him, he couldn't figure out why. He'd been with other women before. A couple of years back, he'd even taken one of them to a wedding that Colleen had also attended.

It was fine. She was fine. Heck, Ike was good with things. None of them expected Beck to live in a box and never venture out.

What was different this time? It wasn't like he was marrying Sidney. Hell, he wasn't even sure what it was exactly they were doing, but they were both adults.

Her admission the night before should have sent up a couple of red flags, at least, but he decided not to think about it and to just take in every moment of this lazy, sunny Sunday morning with a girl whose company he enjoyed.

He supposed they'd be having some sort of talk about this thing between them soon enough. But right now, Beck liked things just the way they were. And besides, just like he'd told Nathan a few days ago when his brother had gotten all up in his business, Sidney was headed back to San Diego. It was where she belonged.

This thing between them had a life expectancy, and though he didn't know her plans—they'd actually never talked about them—he was going to assume the due date was coming soon. How long could she stay away from her business?

So, he'd pushed all that stuff aside and, after breakfast, which was actually more or less a late brunch, they passed by the church once more because he had some measurements to do. Since Jingle was at his place, they picked up Chinese take-out and headed back there, their intention to spend a quiet night in. It just seemed to be the habit they'd fallen into.

Nate had sent at least four text messages asking him to call him back. All of which Beck had ignored on account of him still being annoyed with his brother. They'd just gotten inside and Sidney was unpacking their take-out when his cell pinged again, and she glanced up.

"Who keeps texting you?"

"Nate," he all but growled.

"Why aren't you answering him?" She paused, hand in midair. "What if it's the babies?"

Shit. He'd never thought of that. Beck scooped out his cell

and called his brother at the same time there was a knock on the door. He headed over and yanked it open to find his mother and father and Nana Jacobs standing there with big grins on their faces —well, not his father. Samuel Jacobs looked decidedly uncomfortable.

"Beck?" Nate's voice rang in his ear.

"You're too late," he said, stepping back.

"Oh. Well, next time, answer your damn phone."

Beck pocketed his cell and let his folks have a moment to shed their jackets and boots.

"We haven't seen you in weeks, Beckworth, so I hope you don't mind our unannounced visit." His grandmother smiled up at him.

"No," he replied. "Why would I?"

Hazel Jacobs gave him the kind of hug only a grandmother could, and he then he shook his father's hand before enveloping his mother in a hug as well. He glanced toward the kitchen. "This is my friend, Sid, Nana."

He didn't offer up anything else because he was pretty damn sure Nate would have filled them in on the stuff they wanted to know. Hell, they probably knew more about Sidney Barrett than he did.

She walked over and said hello to his grandmother and then looked at him. She was off balance, he saw that, but her composure was on point. "We could order more Chinese?" She turned back to his parents. "If you like?"

"Oh, no, dear, thanks for asking. We had a late lunch at Nathan's, and we were just on our way home." His mother's gaze settled back on Beck. "Now I know why I haven't seen much of my son." Her gentle, almost teasing words were followed by an awkward silence.

"Oh my," Hazel said. "What have we here?" Jingle stood on the edge of the sofa, meowing and arching her back like a pro, loving the attention she got. His grandmother stroked her back. "This is the kitten I've been hearing about. She's lovely, Beckworth."

"Beer?" he asked his dad, grateful when the man nodded. His mother and grandmother declined, and Sidney already had one open.

The two of them moved to the kitchen, where he grabbed them each a Bud Light. He took a good, long draw and leaned against the island, his eyes on his mother and grandmother and Sidney.

"I told them you were busy." Samuel shook his head. "Said there was a reason you've been scarce of late and that you were a grown man and didn't need a bunch of females poking about your business." His father sighed. "But when your nana heard about Sidney, well, she insisted on coming for a visit."

"Nana?" That surprised Beck. Usually, it was his mother who was the poker.

"She worries about you same as the rest of us."

"Dad, there's nothing to worry about. I'm good."

Samuel nodded. "I see that." And then he grinned. "She seems real nice."

Beck didn't reply. His parents were way too invested in his personal life. He got it. He really did. Didn't mean he had to like it. He finished his beer and dug around for a teakettle when Hazel insisted on a cup before the trip home.

"Sorry, Nan, I don't have sugar cookies or anything to go with it." He flashed a grin and rooted through the fridge. "You're lucky I have milk."

"Tea is fine."

His grandmother steeped her bag and glanced sideways at him.

"Your friend seems lovely," was all she said, and Beck had just about had it.

"Not you too, Nan. Look, I don't know what we're doing here. Sid's great. She really is. But we haven't even had a talk about what this is or what we're doing, and I can't stand that everyone's up in my business and asking questions for things I don't have the answers for. Hell, I haven't figured that out yet."

"That's the fun part, though. The figuring-out part." Hazel Jacobs peered at him over the cup in her hands. In the living room, Sid was deep in conversation with his parents, talking about the church he still hadn't decided on, from what he could hear.

"Being with another woman doesn't mean you loved Cate any less than you remember."

And there it was. The crux of the matter.

He turned around and faced his grandmother. "I don't think I can love anyone else the way I loved her, Nana. It's not possible."

"Oh, my boy." Hazel moved closer and put her hand on his chest. "Every love is different, and you're not meant to love anyone else the same way you loved Cate. You can't, because there's only one Cate." She nodded to the living room. "Just like there's only one Sidney."

"But—"

She shook her head and wouldn't let him finish. "I know what you're thinking, and no, I don't know if you're in love with this woman. But if and when you do fall in love again, Beckworth..." She smiled. "And you will fall in love again. It will be different. One hundred percent different. You're not the young man you were, and life has left its mark on you. It's changed you, and that's going to change the way you love. The thing is, my boy, you need to let it happen. But more importantly, you need to accept it." She finished her tea and set her cup on the counter. "Love is the easy part. It's all the other things that make it hard. It's all the other things you need to let go of."

She cleared her throat in a way that told Beck they were done and stepped around him. "I'm ready to go, Samuel."

His parents followed her lead, and, after all the goodbyes and a couple more hugs, Sidney included, they closed the door behind them and were finally alone.

"Let's eat," he said, and moved to the kitchen.

He warmed up the food while she grabbed some plates, and they sat around the island eating Chinese.

"Your parents must have been close to Cate."

Beck paused, an egg roll halfway to his mouth. "They've known her since she was a kid, so, yeah, they were close. She was like family to them."

"Like you are to her parents."

"I've known them since I was six and her dad coached my hockey team." Beck pushed his plate away and stared straight ahead. His chest was tight, and that feeling that had lingered for days, the one that said all this happiness he'd been enjoying couldn't last, well, it up and hit him square in the face. "Why are we talking about my family? Or Cate, for that matter?"

"Because I want to know about them?" She slid off the stool and took a few steps, watching him warily, those big eyes of her confused. "I shared my darkest secrets with you last night. I guess I feel like I deserve some of yours in return."

He couldn't explain the anger in him. It was just there, big and ugly and making him crazy. He got up and tossed all the leftovers in the garbage.

"I don't feel like sharing, Sid. I didn't know that was in the playbook."

"Playbook? What's that supposed to mean?"

"This. This thing we're doing. What are the rules? Is there a rule that says I need to sit down for an entire evening and tell you that Cate McBride was the love of my life? That the day she died, a part of me went with her? That I miss her so bad sometimes, I wake up in the middle of the night and think she's there with me?" He paced the floor. "Is that what you want to hear?"

"I don't know what I want to hear, Beck. But I do know I don't deserve your attitude or your anger or your flippant disregard for my feelings."

Sid looked hurt, which made him angrier, but not at her —at himself. He was fucking this up royally and had no one to blame but himself.

"Christ, I'm making a mess of this."

She nodded. "You are." She grabbed her jacket and purse and headed for the front door. "Take me back to the cottage. I think maybe some space will be a good thing."

"Come on, Sid." God, he felt like an absolute shit. "Stay." He thought about what his Nana had said. "Let's figure this out."

"Please," she said sharply. "Take me home."

"If that's what you want."

"It is." Her words were clipped, and that was that. Beck grabbed his keys, and, ten minutes later, he sat in his truck, in her driveway, watching her disappear inside the darkened cottage. It was the first night they'd been apart in weeks.

He wasn't sure about a lot of things, but when he got home, he knew one thing for sure. He didn't like that she wasn't there.

CHAPTER EIGHTEEN

At three in the morning, her cell rang. At first, Sid had no idea where she was. It was dark, her brain was fuzzy, and there was a weight on her that she hadn't felt in a long time.

She rolled over and grabbed her cell from the table beside the bed as memories of her fight with Beck rolled around in her brain.

"It's me."

She blinked and sat up, pushing her wild mane of hair away from her face. "Beck? What's wrong?"

"I can't sleep."

She knew the feeling all too well. In fact, she'd only fallen asleep less than an hour earlier.

"You there?" Beck asked, his voice so close, it felt as if he were in the room with her.

"Yes."

"Can I come in?"

Heart beating faster now, she sat up straighter. "Where are you?"

"Look outside."

Sid padded over to the window and pushed aside the blinds. There in a pool of moonlight, staring back up at her, was Beck.

"I meant what I said, Sid. About wanting to figure this out. I just...we have to go slow is all. I need to take things at my own pace, or this isn't going to work. That's me speaking as honestly as I can."

Her heart filled and expanded. She began to shiver so bad, her teeth rattled inside her head.

"You know where the spare key is," she whispered.

She tossed her cell and ran to the bathroom and had just enough time to gargle and run her fingers through her hair. When she came back to the bedroom, he stood there by the bed, watching her, his face half covered by darkness.

Something inside her melted at the sight of him. Some piece of herself that melted and liquefied and filled every inch of her. She didn't need to figure anything out. She knew what she felt. If not before, then right now, standing here with him, there was no doubt.

The struggle would be to keep it inside until the time was right. Until he was ready.

She walked over to him and stood on her tiptoes, smiling hungrily when his hands slid down her body to lift her up and accept her kiss.

And his kiss... Holy hell, the man could kiss.

Her toes curled, her stomach clenched, and when he finally set her back down on her feet, she had to work to breathe properly. She shed her clothes and helped him out of his. There was an urgency to her, a need to connect to him that was fed not only by desire, but, she would think much later, fear.

She touched his chest and moved lower to his abdomen. She loved the way he felt, how he reacted to her. When his hands slid up to either side of her face, she went limp at the look in his eyes. There was no denying the desire he felt for her. His need was as great as her own.

He kissed her again as they fell back onto the bed, his mouth a hot searching thing that suckled and kissed and tugged at the places that drove her crazy. He loved her breasts, then slid to her stomach, to her hips and butt. Then he was urging her knees apart, and his mouth was on her, licking and suckling until she began to tremble.

When she was almost there, he moved up and buried himself with one thrust. They began to move, their bodies attuned to each other on a level she'd never experienced before. Beck's eyes glittered as he looked down at her, and for one moment in time, she thought she saw that thing she'd been waiting for. The thing that meant he felt the same.

He came and collapsed beside her, immediately folding Sid up into his arms. Overcome with emotion and the depth of this connection she felt, she closed her eyes. She thought of the future, of having this feeling for the rest of her life. Of watching Beck laugh, or frown when he was concentrating on something. She thought of how gentle he was with Jingle, and how he'd do anything for his brother or any one of his friends.

He wasn't perfect, of course, he wasn't, but he was the kind of man she wanted. The kind of man she needed.

"I love you."

Horrified at what she'd just done, Sid's eyes flew open. *She'd said the words out loud.* He tensed, and for a moment, all she could hear was her heart beating in her ears, and the sound of wilds thoughts echoing in her brain.

Oh my God, what have I done?

Maybe he didn't hear me.

Is he going to say something?

But Beck didn't say anything. He kept her close, and she felt his warmth at her back all night. Eventually, he fell asleep, but Sid was awake for a long time afterward, because she'd done the thing she'd told herself she wouldn't do.

And he hadn't said it back.

CHAPTER NINETEEN

Sidney woke early, a pillow clutched to her chest, the bed empty. It was that in-between time of half-light, gray shadows, and dreams. Outside, the world was already awake, and the lonely sound of a loon echoed across the lake. The answering chatter of the swallows, blue jays, and cardinals that lived on the property filled the air. She knew if she looked outside the window, she'd see squirrels darting across the lawn, and maybe catch sight of the big owl that lived in the ancient oak out front. With the snow melted, the temperature on the rise, and spring officially arrived, the entire area buzzed with growth and excitement.

Everyone and *everything* felt lighter today...except Sid. She focused on the empty pillow, on the imprint Beck left behind. She closed her eyes and inhaled his scent, and the memory of their lovemaking filled her with bittersweet longing. Her throat tightened as hot tears stung the corners of her eyes. Shit. She'd gone and done the thing she told herself not to do.

She'd said the three words, the ones she thought she'd never utter again, and he hadn't said anything in return. He'd stared at her for so long, fear crept into her heart. But then he'd kissed her so sweetly, so softly, hope had bloomed. They'd made love with an intensity that had left her quaking. She'd thought things were good and settled, until they weren't.

She'd said those three words, and he'd left in the night when he thought she was asleep.

Humiliation made her turn over and bury her face in the pillow; hurt encouraged the tears to come. She'd convinced herself Beck felt the same. Heck, even Molly had said she thought he was falling in love with Sid.

Maybe he was scared. Maybe he was confused. But how was she to know? In these past weeks, he never spoke about his feelings. It was something she understood. The past and all its messiness should stay where it belonged. She even respected it. In some ways, maybe she encouraged the silence, because it was easier for her not to know. Not to think and wonder.

But then she went and fell in love with him, and now the things he kept back were the things she needed to know. To hear and feel and respond to. She said those three words, and he didn't say anything back, and now he was gone, and she was supposed to leave for San Diego in three hours.

She forced herself off the bed and into the shower, moving through the motions of life with two feet stuck firmly in this miserable moment. She packed quickly and ignored the ping of her phone until it drove her to shut it off completely.

Her sister could wait. She'd be seeing her in a few hours anyway.

Sid made the bed and gathered her bags. She left them near the front door and made a pot of coffee. She was about to pour herself a cup to enjoy for the last time on the back deck when a sharp knock and the jangling of the doorknob caught her attention.

Her heart leapt into her chest.

Beck.

She rushed to the front door and yanked it open, only to find her sister standing there, hand raised as if to knock again.

"What the..." Confused, Sid tumbled over her words. "Why are you..." Then, panicked, she got control of herself. "Did something happen to Mom?"

"No. Sorry. Mom is good. I just... I tried to call, but you didn't pick up."

"Why? What are you doing here?"

Kylie lowered her eyes and picked at the cuff of her light jacket. "Can I come in?"

Still confused, Sid stood back and then closed the door behind her sister once she was inside. She headed to the kitchen and grabbed a second mug from the cupboard, filled it, and handed it over to Kylie, who watched in silence.

She added cream and sugar to hers and nodded toward the back. "Follow me. We can have this conversation outside."

The sun enveloped the deck, dappled beams of gold that spread its warmth over the entire area. With no breeze, it was cozy and inviting. Kylie ditched her jacket and sank into one of the chairs, while Sid took the one opposite to her sister.

"You know I'm supposed to leave for the airport in an hour." Sid took a sip of coffee and let the caffeine do its work while her sister nodded.

"I was hoping to catch you before you left."

"Why? This is crazy, you being here." She shook her head. "If Mom's okay, what is it? One of the girls? Did Francine go into early labor?" She felt bad that she hadn't spoken to any of her girlfriends since she'd been in Michigan.

"No. Everything back home is good."

"Is something going on with you?"

Again, her sister said no.

"Okay. Well, you need to explain to me why you felt the need to fly across the country to see me an hour before I leave for my flight home. Which, coincidentally, is in the same city that you live in." Sid didn't bother to keep the sarcasm from her voice, because having any kind of conversation with her sister wasn't something she wanted to deal with. Not when she was still processing everything that had happened the night before.

Kylie sighed and tucked a long piece of ink-black hair behind her ear. She took a drink from her mug and set it on the table.

"I came to make sure you don't ruin your life."

"Excuse me?" Sid had been eyeing the robin on the tree to her right and whipped her head back so fast, she felt her neck crack.

"You heard me."

"I might have heard you, but you sure as hell need to elaborate." She narrowed her eyes. "Just a little bit."

"So, this Beck guy."

"Not talking about him," Sid replied, anger giving her words some depth. "Tell me you did not come all the way out here to talk about some guy I met on vacation."

"I did." Kylie sat up. "I am."

"Well, you wasted your time and a lot of air miles, because I'm not discussing Beck with you."

"Why not?"

God, her sister was relentless

"I don't owe you an explanation."

"Oh, but you do." Kylie got to her feet and sank her hands into the front pockets of her jeans. "Because I love you. And I don't know if it's a twin thing or a sister thing, but what I do know is that when your life sucks, my life sucks. When you're in pain and so low you can't see the way up, I'm the one reaching down to grab you. I'm the one who worries. Who can't think straight until I know you're okay. I'm the one who's there in the middle of the night when you want to talk, and I let you talk until you can't anymore. And then, when you fall asleep because you're spent, I lie awake and worry that I won't be there for the next one." Her chin trembled. "And the thing is, I know you'd be there for me too. You have been. When I flunked out of Columbia and Mason dumped me, I thought my life was over. I was so low, I thought I'd never make it back. You made me see I was being an idiot, and you were there until I made things right. So now I need to know you're going to be okay, because you haven't been okay for a very, very long time, and Sid, it's fucking exhausting."

The tears that had been threatening since before Sid rolled out of bed ran down her face. She sniffled and swiped at them, watching her sister in silence for as long as she could bear it.

"I screwed up, Ky."

"What do you mean?"

Sid shrugged and said simply, "I love him."

"Oh sweetie, that's great. After everything you've been through to find that again, to *love* again, is wonderful." Kylie took a step closer. "Isn't it?"

Sid grabbed up her mug again, if only to have something to hold on to. "I guess it means I'm not dead inside. So there's that. But..."

"But?" her sister prodded.

"He doesn't feel the same. I thought he cared about me the way I do for him, and we...last night, I told him I loved him, and he..." Her voice caught, and she exhaled slowly, trying like hell to keep it together. "He didn't say it back." She whispered the words, hating every syllable.

For a few moments, the only sounds were the birds in the trees and a motorboat off in the distance. Kylie knelt in front of Sid and smiled. "That doesn't mean anything. He could feel the same. You probably took him by surprise is all. Did he leave when you told him?"

Sidney shook her head. "No. We made love. But it was different. It felt different." She thought of his hands and how his eyes held hers as he sank inside her. "It felt like goodbye."

"Did you talk about it?" Kylie asked gently.

"He left in the middle of the night. He thought I was asleep."

"Then you need to go to him. You need to know where he stands."

"No."

"You're being a fraidy-cat." Kylie reached out her hand. "This is why I'm here. I knew you needed me. I knew it last night. I was in the middle of the last episode of *Game of Thrones*, even though I hate the way it ended, but still, Jon Snow, right? Anyway, I got this intense feeling in my gut, and I turned off the TV and booked my flight."

"I appreciate that, but I don't need you."

"Yeah, you do."

"For what, exactly?" Sid glared up at her sister, more than a little pissed off.

"To kick your butt is why. Now take my hand and get out of that chair. You need to go see him before you leave. You'll never forgive yourself if you don't. Life's a crapshoot, Sid. None of us can see around the corner, and we don't know what the future holds. You know that more than anyone. So when something good comes around, you need to hold it close and keep it safe. It's like Frodo with the ring."

"Who?"

"Oh my God. Lord of the Rings? Never mind. Your taste in movies sucks. Don't let this chance at happiness slip through your fingers. There might not be another one."

Sid stared at Kylie's outstretched fingers until her vision blurred. Until her face ached with the effort it took to stop crying. Then she reached forward and let her sister pull her up.

Could she do this? Confront Beck and demand to know where he stood? Ask him why he said nothing when she opened her heart to him?

Could she go on with her life if she didn't?

No.

"Okay," she said, heading back inside. She grabbed her keys and paused at the front door. "Thanks, Ky. For coming and for making me see what I need to do," she said, looking over her shoulder.

"You're welcome, and, Sid?"

"Yes?"

"Cee Cee booked my flight. I used your air miles."

"I figured as much."

Her sister walked over and kissed her cheek. "Make him see what he has if he's brave enough to take it," she whispered, and stepped back. "I'll be here, waiting, because you're stuck with me. Always."

Sidney convinced herself that Beck's truck wouldn't be in the driveway, so when she spied it sitting there, for a moment, she considered driving past his place and forgetting the whole thing. But then she thought of her sister, of the fact she'd flown all the way from San Diego to make sure Sid did what she needed to do, what she had to do, really, and she pulled in behind him. She slid from her rental before she could change her mind and knocked on his door.

Beck opened it before she had a chance to knock again. His hair was a mess, his jaw shadowed with two days' worth of beard, and he was dressed in faded jeans and nothing else. His expression was serious, his eyes soft, and they melted her heart without even trying.

"Hey," he said slowly, moving aside to give her room to enter.

Jingle meowed from the counter and jumped onto the chair,

watching them both with her little head to the side, those green eyes of hers blinking slowly as she did so.

"I was just getting dressed to come over," Beck said, shoving his hands into the front pockets of his jeans.

"Why did you leave?" She asked the question even though she was damn scared to hear the answer. She watched him closely, watched the play of emotion on his face, and her stomach fell. He was going to break her heart, and this time, she wasn't going to be able to put it back together.

"I couldn't sleep," he replied.

"Why?"

He eyed her, and she saw the hesitation. He didn't want to hurt her.

"Just say it, Beck. Is it because of what I said? Those three words no guy wants to hear unless he feels the same?"

He swore under his breath and looked up at the ceiling. She knew he was conflicted and in pain. This wasn't easy for him, and it sure as hell didn't make it easier for her. She had to say what was in her heart. It was the only way she could move forward.

"I came to Crystal Lake because I was in a bad place and knew I was too close to the edge of something even darker. After the miscarriage and Nick's cheating and our breakup, I wanted to crawl inside myself and never come out. This place, the people here, you especially, made me want to live again. I wasn't looking for this to happen, Beck. Honestly, I didn't think I would feel this way again. Not in this lifetime. But it did happen, and..." She had to take a moment because she couldn't break down, not now. "I love you," she whispered. "That's not going to change, and I need you to know that. But I also need you to know I can't say those three words and get nothing back. I can't."

Sidney took those last remaining steps until she was inches

from him. She placed her hands on his chest, felt his heart beat strong beneath her touch, and fought the urge to bury herself in his neck.

"You need to tell me what's in your heart."

Slowly, Beck's hands crept up until he held her face prisoner. For the longest time, he said nothing, and when he finally spoke, his voice was husky.

"You're an amazing woman who deserves the kind of man who's all in. I can't give you that, and, man, I wish I could. My heart isn't whole. It's missing pieces I'll never get back, and you deserve so much more. Cate's still a thing for me. And I know it's stupid and a lot of folks would say I'm crazy. A selfish man would make a go of it, but I can't do that to you. I do love you, Sid. You need to know that, but..."

She attempted a smile. "You don't love me enough."

"I..." He swore again and dropped his hands, turning away. "I never wanted to hurt you."

Oh, but he had. She was crushed, and it took everything Sid had to keep her noodle legs from crumpling beneath her.

She took a step back and looked to the table where Cate's picture still stood. Tragic Cate, who'd been gone over ten years and still had a hold on Beck. She must have been something fierce. Sid looked at the man who held her heart in his hands, and then back to Cate, who existed somewhere else entirely.

"I'm not sorry this happened, and I don't regret meeting you. I hope someday, her ghost lets you go."

Blinking back tears, Sidney pushed her way outside and made it back to her vehicle. She didn't remember driving back to the cottage, but suddenly, she was there inside the beautiful stone cottage she'd come to love, and Kylie was in front of her.

She didn't say a word, not even when Kylie pulled her into a hug and held her close.

"Let's go home," her sister said. "Everything will be okay. I promise."

Sidney grabbed up her bags and walked out into the Michigan sunshine for the last time. Things weren't okay, but she would survive.

She always did.

CHAPTER TWENTY

By early May, spring settled over Crystal Lake with a surprising heat that encouraged backyard barbecues, picnics at the lake, boating out to Pottahawk Island, and quiet mornings fishing from the dock. For most folks, anyway. For Beck? It meant longer hours, and he immersed himself in his work.

He got up before light, went for a run, then worked until dusk. When his pals asked about all the hours he spent on his current project, an old church on the outskirts of town he was converting into a home, he just shrugged and said he had a deadline to keep.

The deadline was bullshit, but it was enough to keep most of them out of his business. Except family, of course. Lately, he'd spent more time avoiding his mother than he would like, but ever since Sid left town, she'd ramped up her concern and the need to let him know he'd made the biggest mistake of his life.

Take this morning, for instance. She was waiting for him on his porch when he'd gotten back from his run, Jingle on her lap purring like the little traitor she was. His mother didn't say anything at first. She followed him inside and made coffee while he had a quick shower. Afterward, they talked about nothing that mattered while having coffee on the porch. Beck actually thought he'd come out on the lucky side of things and avoided a lecture, but just as she was about to leave, she turned to him, and the look on her face told him otherwise.

"One day, you'll have children and understand. I'll worry about you and Nate until I take my last breath. It's part of being a parent."

He knew she meant well, and she *was* his mother, so Beck kept silent. Jingle rubbed against his legs and flopped onto her back, purring madly as she stared up at him, long tail swishing, front paws kneading his ankle. For a second, it was all he heard, but then his mother was in front of him, a sad smile tugging at her mouth. Regret or something close to it clouded her eyes.

"I wish I could have shielded you from what happened with Cate, but life doesn't work that way. I know you loved her, and I know it was the kind of love most folks dream about. I just don't want you to close yourself off from the possibility of it happening again."

"Mom," he said quietly. "We've been through this."

"I know," she whispered. "But please promise me something?"

"Sure," he said with a slight nod.

"Don't stay stuck where you are because of a sense of loyalty. Cate wouldn't want that."

She stood on her tiptoes and kissed his cheek, and that was it. Her words haunted him all day.

Beck tossed his hammer and stood back from the wall he'd just framed. Sweat rolled off him, and he scooped up the towel he kept nearby and swabbed at his face and neck before grabbing his big thermos of water. It was close to five o'clock on a Saturday, and he was supposed to be at Nate's for a family barbecue/baby shower by six. He took a long drink and, though he'd prefer to work until dark, knew that if he didn't show his face, it would only encourage more unwanted visits from his mother and anyone else who felt like poking their nose in his business.

He locked up the place, hopped into his truck, and, less than fifteen minutes later, was in the shower. It didn't take him long to get ready, and he pulled on a plain white T-shirt and a pair of khaki shorts. He topped up Jingle's food and water bowls, though the growing kitten wasn't interested in food. She wanted to play and swiped at him when he walked by her. He scratched her belly and then behind her ears, and was about to head outside when his cell rang. It was Nate, who'd forgotten to pick up a cake at the grocery store. Their parents were already at his place, so Beck agreed to grab it for them.

Crystal Lake was busy, as was the grocery store, and he had to park across the street from it. It was a small, family-run operation, and though there was a new, larger store in the development across the lake, the Jacobs were townies and still preferred to shop here.

He nodded to Mrs. Avery the florist on his way in and grabbed a cart since there were three additional text messages from his brother. Shit. People said women had pregnancy brain? Nate was a mess.

Beck grabbed two cases of soda as well as ketchup, mustard, and relish. Then he headed to the produce section and tossed in two large onions, three tomatoes, and a head of lettuce before pointing his cart in the direction of the bakery counter, where Mr. Gilroy, the man who'd run the bakery section since Beck was a kid, had the cake ready.

By the time he got back to the checkout line, which was

busy, and paid for everything, it was six thirty and his stomach was rumbling. He'd just stowed the groceries and cake in his truck and was about to take the cart back to the store when he glanced up and locked eyes with Colleen McBride, Cate's mother. He hadn't seen Colleen since that night on the river when he and Sid had crossed paths with her.

She smiled and walked toward him, accepting his hug and returning it with warmth and familiarity. He'd been a part of her family since he was a horny teenager trying to get into her daughter's pants. After Cate's tragic passing, she'd never let go.

Colleen peered through the window into his truck and smiled. "That cake must be for Molly and Nathan. Mr. Gilroy has outdone himself."

"I'm headed there now."

Colleen nodded. "When is Molly's due date?"

"Couple weeks? I think?" Beck answered sheepishly because it felt wrong that he didn't know the exact date. "Can't come any sooner. Nate's driving everyone crazy."

The two of them made small talk for a bit. He asked after Ben, Cate's father, and she wondered how his grandmother was doing. She mentioned the new development across the river and the fact that so much building was going on, and he told her he was sticking to renovating on this side. She asked about the Somers' home he'd recently finished, and he told her about the old church he'd bought. They talked about all the things a person talked about when you didn't want to discuss that one thing that you should. And when he gave her a hug and said he better get his butt in gear, Colleen slowly nodded, but she didn't let go.

She stared up into his eyes for a long time, long enough that the two of them drew the attention of an older couple packing away their groceries.

"That girl you were with the last time I saw you. What

happened to her?" She spoke haltingly and slowly let her hands fall away.

Beck's gaze dropped, and he exhaled. "She went back to San Diego. It's where she lives."

"Really? I'm surprised."

He yanked up his head. "What do you mean?"

Colleen's chin trembled a bit, but she didn't take her eyes from him. She swallowed thickly, as if working up the courage to speak, and when she did, her voice was filled with emotion. "She looked at you the way Cate used to. And you..." She stumbled over her words and shook her head as if angry with herself. Or him. Or the world. "You looked at her the same way."

"Colleen," Beck interrupted her. He couldn't do this. Not with her. Not now.

"No. You need to listen to me, Beck, because it's okay. It's more than okay." A soft smile lightened her face. "My daughter loved you very much. As young as she was, you were her world. But she's gone, and nothing will change that or what the two of you had. She would want you to be happy, and I think she'd be upset if she knew you were hiding from the future because you keep looking to the past."

"Colleen, that's not me."

"Isn't it? You've been alone since she left us, and you're a young man, Beckworth. Too young. I don't want that for you, and neither would Cate." She stepped back, her heart shining from her eyes. "Don't be afraid to love again. Be brave and embrace it. If not for yourself, then for Cate, because she's not here and she won't have the chance. Ever."

His eyes felt wet. He swiped at the corners, though he remained silent.

Colleen reached for his empty cart and, with one last look, headed for the grocery store.

Beck drove all the way to his brother's place with the radio cranked because he needed the distraction. His heart thudded against his chest, a fast staccato that filled his ears and made him anxious. By the time he reached the Manchester house, he was buzzing with nervous energy.

There were several cars parked in the driveway, and he figured it was a full house. Molly and Nate had a wide assortment of friends. He slipped inside and headed for the kitchen, setting down his bags and the cake before returning to his truck for the soda. Once that was stashed in the fridge, he walked to the extra-wide garden doors and stood there for a few moments.

The deck was decorated in pink and blue balloons, with streamers blowing in the wind. His mom sat on his dad's lap, her arm draped casually around his shoulders as he told one of his stories. Nate and Molly listened, along with her brother Zach and his wife, Jess, Molly's parents and Beck's grandmother, Hazel. The gang was there as well, guys they'd grown up with and the women they'd started families with. His dad's story must be a good one, because everyone's eyes were on him and there was much laughter.

Beck felt like the outsider he'd become over these last few years. Always looking in from the outside, that piece of the puzzle that was warped and no longer fit. Some ghost of a feeling had settled in his gut somewhere between the grocery store and his brother's place. It was cold and dark and filled him with fear. It was something more than loneliness and had the bitter taste of regret.

He watched Nate lean over and kiss Molly, his hand on her large belly, heavy with the life they'd created together. He'd wanted that once. A wife and a couple of kids, and then it had disappeared in the cold reality of Cate's death.

And yet...hadn't it come back to life?

He thought of Sid and the way she bit her bottom lip when she concentrated, or how she twirled a piece of hair when she was nervous. How she laughed with no boundaries, a great big belly of a thing that filled a room with sunshine. He remembered the way her eyes darkened when he was inside her, how her hands dug in hard as if she was never letting go. And how it felt to hold her when she opened up and told him about the things that had nearly destroyed her.

She'd trusted him. *She'd loved him.* And he'd let her slip away. He'd stood there, that day she'd come to him, and let her walk out of his home. What the fuck was wrong with him?

He clenched his hands and took a step back from the blissful scene on the deck as realization hit. HIs actions weren't about Cate, which was what he'd always thought. It was about self-preservation. About protecting himself from that kind of hurt again. He was a coward hiding behind the ghost of a dead woman.

Ashamed, Beck dropped his head into his hands and turned away from the garden door. Christ, he'd made a mess of things.

I love her.

Just then, Nate walked into the house.

"Hey, I didn't know you were here. You need a beer?" Nate walked past him and headed for the kitchen. "I've got to find the big barbecue utensils. Apparently, I didn't put them back where they're supposed to go. Molly says I do it all the time, but I didn't want to tell her she's the one who used the barbecue last time. Might send her over the edge. So where the hell would she put them?" Nate glanced up and frowned. "Are you okay?"

"I don't know."

Nate closed the drawer he'd been searching through and walked over to Beck. "What's going on?"

"I'm an idiot."

"Well, yeah, but what's going on?" Nate attempted a smile, but it fell flat. "You don't look okay."

"I screwed everything up."

"Are we talking about the grocery order? 'Cause if you forgot the ketchup, Molly will blow a gasket. She eats ketchup sandwiches, for God's sake. It's the grossest thing I've ever seen. I've had to cross the border twice in the last month alone to buy ketchup chips in Canada. Honestly, those babies are going to pop out with red hair and red skin. You wait and see."

"I got the ketchup."

Nate nailed him with a knowing look. "This is about Sid."

"She told me she loved me," Beck bit out. "And I let her walk away." He looked his brother straight in the eye. "I didn't realize until just now that I feel the same."

"I could have told you weeks ago but Molly said you needed to figure it out on your own. Not that I didn't try, but hell, you've been the worst kind of bastard lately. All of us could see it, and none of us could say anything because anytime anyone brought up Sid, you damn near bit our heads off."

Beck looked away. His brother was right. He'd been an outright asshole.

"What are you going to do about it?"

Beck yanked his head around. "What do you mean?"

"I'm just saying you need to nail this down, and the sooner the better. Sidney Barrett isn't going to be waiting forever. Hell, it might already be too late. You need a grand gesture. Something big to make up for being such an absolute bastard."

"Don't hold back, Nate," he muttered darkly.

His brother swore. "You hurt her bad."

He was right, but Beck had to look to the future and hope that the past could be forgotten. He looked outside once more, his mind already turning, his body already in motion.

"Tell Molly I'm sorry I missed the shower."

"Just don't miss the birth, or there'll be hell to pay." Nate smiled widely, as if pleased with the turn of events. "Anything else?"

Beck paused at the door. "Text me Sid's sister's cell number and Sid's address in San Diego."

"You got it. And Beck?"

He glanced over his shoulder.

"Don't screw this up."

CHAPTER TWENTY-ONE

It was raining. Sid swore and strode across the parking lot, headed to the space she leased for her business. It hardly ever rained in San Diego, and today she needed sunshine for the photo shoot they had planned on the boardwalk. She glanced up at the steel-gray sky and sighed. It wasn't looking good.

The old warehouse had been converted into office space several years back. She walked inside, took the elevator up to the top floor, and said hello to Mattie, the young receptionist she'd hired months ago. The girl was fresh out of college, an eager learner, and there was always a smile on her face.

"Derek says he thinks we can delay the shoot by a couple hours. I checked, and this rain is supposed to move off by noon, so he's on his way down to the water to set up as soon as it does. The photographer is with him and a few staff to help with that."

The sky she'd just seen didn't seem as enthusiastic at the thought of disappearing, but Sid gave a quick smile and headed toward her office. As her brand, Barrett Lifestyle, grew, she'd moved from an office building downtown to this place, where she'd secured the entire top floor of the old warehouse. It was huge, well over ten thousand square feet. With only three offices fully enclosed, as well as a conference room along the right side, the rest of the space was open, with several workstations for staff and various spaces for filming videos, including a state-of-the-art kitchen, a bedroom, a cozy fireplace with inviting furniture, a gym, and a large bedroom complete with a makeup area for tutorials. On the floor below was new space she'd leased just a few weeks ago, and she planned on featuring carpentry projects to complement their home décor segments. She was looking to partner with a local carpenter for a feature she planned to incorporate within six months.

Building her brand was the only thing she cared about these days. It kept her busy and focused, but more importantly, it allowed her to put Beck in a box and forget about him and Crystal Lake. Maybe someday she'd pull it out for a look, but that day would be a long time coming. The pain was still too fresh.

Her office walls were glass, as were the others. She'd loved the concept, and most of the time, she liked to be able to look out at the space and see what everyone was up to, but sometimes, like today, she wished she had a bit more privacy. Sure, she could hit the remote and make the privacy blinds ease over the glass walls, but truthfully, she felt more conspicuous when she did that. As if she was hiding something.

Sid tossed her jean jacket onto the overstuffed chair to her right, closed the door behind her, and wandered over to the floor-to-ceiling windows that overlooked a park across from the warehouse. The sky was still cloud heavy, and that dull gray color did nothing to make Sidney think the photoshoot would go ahead as planned.

She'd recently partnered with a well-known celebrity from

LA and had agreed to model shapewear for a fall campaign. The idea was to pose for pictures along the boardwalk and marina, having a latte at Coffee Bean or gazing out at the water.

She noticed a young mother pushing a stroller and made a mental note to call Molly. She was due any day, and Sid felt bad that they hadn't spoken since she left Crystal Lake. The mother-to-be was busy, of course, but Sid had no excuse other than the fact she'd tried to forget about her time there, at least for a little while.

Her heart constricted at the thought, and she shook her head with a sigh before turning to her desk. Beck was never far from her thoughts.

Her cell rang. She fished it from her purse before sliding onto the chair behind her desk. She leaned back and rolled her neck.

"Hey," her sister said, sounding out of breath.

"Where are you?" Sid hadn't seen her when she arrived.

"On my way in. I just wanted to make sure you were there."

"Where else would I be?"

"The weather looks like shit, so I thought you might decide to cancel the shoot."

Sid eyed the pile of shapewear on the table across from her. "No, Derek says the weather will clear, so we're postponing a couple of hours. I could use your help deciding what to wear."

"Sure," she replied lightly. "Sounds cool."

Sidney could almost picture the wide smile and laughing eyes. She frowned. "You sound like you just inhaled sunshine or something." She sat straighter. "You've got a new man."

"You think I need a man to be in a good mood? Geez, did I miss the memo that said we've transported back to medieval times? Can't I just be happy?"

"No. You can't. You're only happy when you're meddling in

my business or when you've met someone. Since I have no business to meddle with, I say you've met a new guy. Who is he?"

"Okay, you've got me. You know how we've been searching for a new carpenter guy for the new segment? Well, I found him. He's tall and dark and hot in that quiet, deep kind of way. You know, like he's broken and needs to be fixed? I can't wait for you to meet him."

"I'm not interested in fixing anyone."

"Trust me, you're going to want to meet this guy."

Sid sighed because there was no point in arguing with Kylie. She always got her way. "Put him in my calendar. I might have time next week. We'll talk about it when you get in."

"Yeah. We will." Her sister laughed, and then swore at about the same time Sid heard a *horn honk.* Kylie was a notoriously bad driver.

Sid hung up before Kylie could get another word in and wandered over to the table, her fingers smoothing out the various pieces of shapewear. The material was light, the texture silky, and the elasticity and compression impressive. They came in several different shades, from off-white and cream to taupe, brown, and black. She had a feeling the pieces would sell out quickly, and Sid's eye was never wrong.

Now, which ones to wear?

As Sid got busy deciding on the pieces she'd wear for the shoot, a few things were happening she wasn't aware of. With her back turned to the windows, she didn't notice the single beam of light that cut through the rain-heavy sky. It shone down like a beacon and settled on an empty parking spot that was soon filled by none other than her sister in her little red Volkswagen.

She didn't see Kylie drive into the lot as if the hounds of hell were on her heels and pull up with a screech, cutting the engine before the car came to a full stop. And she definitely didn't see the man beside her. He shed his seat belt and got out of the car, eyes on the doors that led inside. He didn't hesitate. He strode forward, a determined look in his eyes, his long legs eating up the distance in no time, and her sister running to catch up.

As Sid put in her wireless earbuds and listened to Tyler Childers, a new favorite, she held up one of the pieces and tried to concentrate on the task at hand, unaware that the same tall, dark, and determined man who'd arrived with her sister stepped off the elevator at the other end of the floor and paused. He wore faded the jeans, a plain white T-shirt underneath a worn black leather jacket. His dark hair was longer than before, and stubble shadowed his jaw, giving him an air of danger he wore well. He focused on the office at the other end of the large, open room, his dark eyes intense in his handsome face.

He was a compelling male specimen, a handsome stranger with an air of mystery, the kind of man who wore his masculinity without thought. Outnumbered in a room full of women, he barely gave them a cursory look before returning his gaze to the large office.

The receptionist, Mattie, nearly dropped a double vanilla latte in her lap when he glanced over and gave a quick nod as if to say *you can't stop me*. As it was, his appearance was so unexpected, his maleness so overwhelming, that she uttered a weird squeaky noise and sank back into her chair as he moved by with purpose.

Jess, who was busy testing a new quinoa recipe in the kitchen, nearly dropped a ceramic bowl when she caught sight of him. He was literally her fantasy come to life. And Bernadette sank into one of the chairs in the living room, where'd she'd been busy arranging an array of throws for a photo shoot planned for a fall launch as he strode past her. She watched him until she had to crank her neck to see where he was headed.

The dark-haired stranger walked with purpose, never wavering from the path that led from the elevator to the glass-walled office. He walked past several assistants, all frozen and curious and more than a little excited, as if they sensed some kind of significant event was about to take place.

They could have asked Kylie, but she would have told them to keep watching. She followed in his footsteps a few paces behind, and, after a few seconds, so did the others. When he reached the office, they paused, silent and anxious. As Sidney pulled on the edge of the shapewear, trying to see how far it would stretch, he reached for the door. And when Tyler sang about his broken heart and the need to shake the frost from his bones, she paused, a whisper of electricity touching her skin as a shiver rolled over her.

She looked out the window and noticed the beam of light, and thought that maybe, after all this rain and gloom, there was hope for her photo shoot after all.

And then she froze as that whisper of electricity solidified into something very real. It crept over her like a secret until she trembled from the weight of it. Her insides liquefied at about the same time the air in her lungs expanded.

What the...

Heat flushed her whole. A mouth on her nape, warm hands on her hips; a mouth and a touch she'd know anywhere.

Heart nearly beating out of her chest and mouth suddenly dry, she set down the shapewear and pulled her earbuds out. She took a moment because her knees were like jelly and she was afraid she'd melt into a puddle of want and need and despair.

Sidney slowly turned around, breath caught in her throat as she locked eyes on the man who'd haunted her dreams for weeks. She inhaled that woodsy fresh scent that was all him and bit her lip because tears stung the corners of her eyes, and she didn't want to cry. Not now. She'd shed too many tears.

But what to say to him?

Why are you here? Can you see past my skin and bones to my broken heart with those laser-sure eyes?

She heard the words inside her mind and opened her mouth to ask them, but Beck shook his head and leaned closer. He didn't give her a chance to do or say anything. He cupped her head between his hands, his eyes not wavering from hers, and whispered, "I love you, Sidney Barrett." His breath was warm against her skin, and his words were thick, filled with emotion. "I let you leave thinking that I didn't love you enough. And for that, I'm sorry, because I was so fucking wrong. I love you *enough*."

He enunciated the word and said it slowly, so there was no way Sid could misunderstand his meaning. Those jelly knees of hers knocked together so hard, his hands were the only things that kept her standing. She grabbed his arms for support, afraid to speak or cry or laugh or do anything. As it turns out, she didn't have to do anything. Beck wasn't finished.

"I love you more than enough. I love the quiet moments we have. I love the way you bite your bottom lip when you're thinking about stuff. I love the smell of your hair, the taste of your body, and the way you sigh when I'm inside you. I love how you like to argue and challenge me and put me in my place when I'm being an asshole."

Beck exhaled a long, shaky breath. "The thing is, Sid, you kind of snuck up on me when I wasn't looking. I'd become used to the idea that there would never be a me and someone else. I hid behind that idea because I was too much of a coward to consider the possibility I was wrong. What I had with Cate was wonderful. But it's in the past and I'm done being stuck back there."

Her eyes were filled with tears, and his face was a blur, but his words, oh how sweet they were.

"But then you came along, this woman I who knocked me off my socks, and I didn't know how much I needed you, how much I loved you until you were gone. There is no one else for me, and I'm done being alone. Everything circles back to you." He rested his forehead against hers. "I love you enough," he said roughly. "And I can love you enough for the both of us. Please tell me I didn't screw this up. Tell me I'm not too late."

Sid couldn't speak. Literally. Her heart was beating so damn fast and her lungs were so constricted, she could barely keep herself upright.

"Sid?" She saw the concern in his eyes, and maybe the fear. Or was it just a reflection of her own? "Can you say something?" he asked roughly.

"Can you just kiss me?"

She barely got the words out before his mouth was on hers. He kissed her until her head spun. Until those jelly knees of hers wobbled together and he had to pick her up or she'd be on the floor. As he held her close, she'd never felt so loved or protected.

"I love you," he murmured against her cheek.

"Enough," she replied huskily.

"More than enough." He nipped at her neck and grinned. "Can we get out of here so I can show you?"

Just then, the door opened behind them, and he turned, cradling Sid in his arms as they faced her entire staff, just outside her office.

Kylie said with a huge grin, "I told you my carpenter was hot."

"You did," Sid replied.

"I think you should hire him."

"I might."

"I, ah, uh...I called Derek and told him to reschedule the shoot. Said you had an unexpected emergency come up and would be out all afternoon."

Sidney was unavailable for close to a week because Beck spent the entire time showing her exactly how much he loved her.

And as it turned out, it was more than enough.

EPILOGUE

"What do you think?"

Beck stood back and watched Sid slowly make her way around the cavernous church. He'd gutted it weeks ago and had finished framing the new layout before his trip to San Diego. Now he was seeing it through her eyes and was anxious for a reaction.

Light filtered through the huge stained-glass windows. As she stood in its circle, he felt his chest tighten and his heart speed up. God, he loved her. Every single thing.

She was dressed simply in a plain blue dress, cream cardigan, and flats. Her hair was bundled on top of her head in a loose bun, her big dark eyes luminous as she turned in a full circle.

"I love it," she said softly, turning to him with a smile. "It's perfect."

He moved to her and pointed to the loft. "That's our bedroom. Kitchen over here and living area there. Back along the right will be a couple more bedrooms, and if you walk through that door over there, it opens to another room where you can work."

"You've thought of everything," she said, reaching for him.

"I tried to." He flashed a grin and pulled her close. "The outbuilding, I'll eventually convert to my workshop, and we've got two acres of land to play with."

"How many bedrooms?" she asked, resting her cheek against his chest.

"Three in addition to ours."

"That sounds about right," she murmured, tilting her chin upward. "We can fill them with lots of babies."

"We can." He nuzzled her neck and felt her breath quicken. "It's a lot of work, though." He nipped at her and moved to her mouth. "Making them, I mean."

"Work?" Her voice was low and throaty. "I think practice is a better word, don't you?"

"Yeah, that's it." He tugged at her bottom lip. "Practice."

"Maybe we should start some of that practicing," she said, reaching for the edge of his T-shirt.

"Maybe we should." Already painfully hard with need, he helped her out and tossed his shirt. Her hands were at his zipper, and, in less time than it took to undo his jeans, the length of him was inside her hot, wet mouth, and he nearly lost his mind.

"Jesus, Sid," he growled, and reached for her. The floor had to be hard on her knees. But she shooed his hands away, and he closed his eyes, loving the way she loved him. She suckled and stroked, and it took a lot just to keep his shit together. When he couldn't stand the pressure anymore, he gently withdrew and doffed his jeans and boots, while she slipped out of her dress.

He yanked on her panties, and they joined the pile of clothes on the floor while he scooped her up, along with her dress, and settled her ass on the blue fabric, which he laid out on his workbench. She immediately opened her legs wide, and, with one thrust, he was deep inside the woman he loved.

He braced her back with one arm, while the other held her hip.

As he thrust inside her slowly, he dipped his head and suckled her nipples, smiling when she arched her back and began to pant. Her hands dug into his back, and she urged him on. She didn't have to ask twice.

"I can't wait," she whispered hoarsely.

Beck loved her thoroughly, his body aching for release. Sweat pooled on his skin as he held off, waiting for the perfect moment. He felt her tighten around him, saw her throat constrict as she whimpered, and, with one more thrust, they came together.

He held her for a long time, long enough for the shakes to subside and for her body to relax.

"That was..." she said, shaking her head.

"Yeah." He kissed the side of her neck. "It was."

"Thing is," she said, returning his kiss with one of her own. "I think there's room for improvement."

He grinned. "You might be right about that."

"We might have to get some more of that practicing in."

"Sounds like a plan." He tugged on a nipple. "We should go see Nate and Molly and the babies before this gets out of hand, though. They were expecting us an hour ago."

"You're right."

Sid held on and didn't let go of him. Her mouth was bruised from his kisses, her skin flushed from their lovemaking, and she was the most beautiful thing he'd ever seen. Beck felt like the luckiest man on the planet. He'd managed to find love again with a woman who completed him body and soul. All the things he thought he'd never have—family, children and love—stared him in the eye, and he was humbled by the enormity of it all.

He was a lucky son of a bitch, and he knew it.

"I love you," he said, dropping one last kiss on her shoulder.

"Enough," she replied with a soft grin.

"More than enough," he growled.

"I'm so looking forward to a life here with you. In this place. And I hope with all this practicing, we'll have a family of our own sooner rather than later." Her breath hitched, and she folded into his arms. "Thank you for coming after me."

After they got dressed, Beck locked up the church. He grabbed her hand and held it while they slowly walked the long driveway to where he'd parked his truck. The sun was shining, the air fresh and warm, and here in his own corner of paradise, Beck finally found his place.

His life was no longer an unfinished puzzle, because all the pieces fit together perfectly, and with Sid at his side, he felt like he could face anything.

Life is good, he thought.

Life is good.

LOVE ME FOREVER

Coming July 2020

The summer Poppy Fairbanks turned sixteen she gave Boone Avery her virginity and he stole her heart. For a few blissful months she walked on clouds, until he left Crystal Lake without a word and she never saw him again. The fact that he's back shouldn't matter. But it does. And she finds herself thinking about that summer, about his hot kisses and what if...

Considering she vowed never to speak to him again, how inconvenient is that?

Boone Avery came back to Crystal Lake to raise his son. As a man who's lived his life for everyone but himself, he's hoping this time around he can do things right. He has no time for romancing a woman, hell, he's still trying to figure out his own life. But what's a guy to do when the one that got away is standing right in front of him? Especially when she makes it clear she doesn't like him all that much.

If you're Boone Avery you throw out the playbook and set your own rules, and to hell with consequence.

I've had a lot of emails about our Poppy, so I hope you enjoy her upcoming book! You can page through to preorder your copy!

And for fans of the Barker Triplets, coming May 2020**, Long Road Home**. What happens after Happy Ever After?

At the age of thirty-six, Bobbi Jo Barker is in a place she thought she'd never be—separated from the only man she'll ever love. Disillusioned, she leaves her home to spend the summer in Louisiana, hoping the heat will heal her broken heart. It doesn't take long to find out that running away makes things worse, and the secret she carries just might bury her.

Shane Gallagher has lost everything that mattered to him. Again. When his sister surprises him with a trip to a B&B in Belle Adair, Louisiana, he takes it, if only to get away, to paint and clear his head. What he doesn't expect to find is his estranged wife staying in the room above him. The undeniable pull that exists between them used to be enough, but life has a way of demanding more.

As days pass into weeks, Bobbi and Shane will have to remember the past in order to fight for their future, and hope the long road home leads to each other.

I've been wanting to revisit this couple for years now, and finally had the time to do so. I hope you enjoy Bobbi and Shane's continuation. For more information, page through.

ABOUT THE AUTHOR

USA Today bestselling author and 2015 RITA® winner JULIANA STONE fell in love with books in the fifth grade when her teacher introduced her to Tom Sawyer. A tomboy at heart, she splits her time between baseball, books, and music. She's thrilled to be writing young adult as well as adult contemporary romance—books that have garnered starred reviews from *Publishers Weekly* & Booklist—from somewhere in the wilds of Canada.

I love hearing from my readers, and you can find me by clicking the links below! If you want to stay abreast of all happenings, you can sign up for my newsletter

http://www.julianastone.com/contact/

Lastly, if you have the time to leave an honest review of my books at point of purchase, or Goodreads, it would be much appreciated! Every little bit helps!

Xo

Juliana

Please visit me at the my website.
www.julianastone.com
or write to me with this email address
juliana@julianastone.com
All other social media links are below!

ALSO BY JULIANA STONE

A Crystal Lake Novel

The Thing About Trouble

That Thing You Do

A Little Bit Of Christmas

Love And Other Things

Love Me Forever

The Blackwells of Crystal Lake

You Make Me Weak - Free

You Drive Me Crazy

You Rock My World

You Own My Heart

The Family Simon series

Tucker -Free

Jack

Maverick

Teague

Grace

Cooper

The Barker Triplets

Offside - Free

Collide

Conceal

A Barker Family Christmas

Long Road Home

Standalone Novels

He's All that

Printed in Great Britain
by Amazon

33276142R00108